Ken

"Damn bitch. Suck that dick just like that," I had a
fist full of hair in my hand while getting some good ass top. I
could hear my phone blowing up but that shit would have to
wait a second. This nut was way past due. Actually, I just got
some pussy this morning but it was past lunch so a new nut
was what I needed. My phone kept going off annoying the
fuck out of me so I just answered it.

"Yoooo," I dragged out my yo' because this head was
good as fuck.

"Really Yatta?! AHHHHH!" I nutted all on this
stupid bitch face. If she would have just focused on sucking
dick she wouldn't have nut all in her lashes. I didn't make the
shit no better. I jacked my dick off shooting the rest of my
load all in her face.

"Ughhhhhh!" Looking down as I emptied my dick I
slapped her stupid ass in the face with it and got up from the
couch.

"YATTA! MY MAKE-UP AND LASHES ARE
RUNIED!" Her stupid ass yelled while running to the
bathroom. I was cracking up while picking up her shirt and
wiping my dick off. I picked up my phone and resumed my
call.

"Yo' who dis?"

"It's me, Ebony, you coming over tonight?" I had to
think for a second and put a face to who I was talking to.

"Ebony? Where I know you from ma?" Standing in
the middle of this bitch living room I was putting on my King
James 15's and looking for my fitted hat.

"Dang how you forget about me already. You gave
me your number at Footlocker today," she had the nerve to
have a little attitude. I still couldn't find her face.

"Oh, you the gap tooth bitch with the fat ass. I
remember you now lil' mama. Look I'll hit you up later

about that," I didn't even give her a chance to say shit before I hung up.

"Um, what the fuck Yatta! I know you wasn't talking to another bitch like I'm not even here," I looked from my phone and back at Cleo dumb ass face.

"Bitch lower your voice before you wake my fucking son up. And do you think I give a fuck about you being in my face. We ain't together and never will be I don't even fuck yo' trick ass. Move tha fuck out tha way," I pushed her by her big ass head and went to the second bedroom in her apartment. Opening the door I peeked in on K.J. and saw my baby boy sound asleep. My baby boy was chunky as hell and at ten months, he was my twin. I kissed his big jaws and went back to looking at him. I had missed the first ten months of his life being locked up in Macomb Correctional Facility. Pigs tried to place me at a murder scene over this dirty ass Grand Rapids nigga. He owed me some money and was playing around. I caught up to him and it was lights out.

He had a family who wouldn't shut the fuck up and keep my name out their mouth. I was arrested a day after my son was born. Shit fucked me up but I remained G about my shit. My stupid ass baby mama didn't even bring my son to see me once. But because I loved the fuck out of him I made sure my niggas kept her rent and bills paid. This bitch wouldn't even let my uncle and his wife see my son. She was throwing a full-blown fit talkin' about I left her lonely. Hoe we were never together! Shit made me burn with anger every time I thought about the shit. I was released yesterday morning and I vowed to never miss a minute of my son life again.

"So what'chu about to go see another bitch-----," I cut the bitch off by grabbing a fist full of her fucking braids.

"Look bitch, don't no fucking body tell me what the fuck to do. I am not your muthafucking business nor is my ten-inch dick yo' fuckin' business. The only thing you need to worry about is my fucking son who you better have ready tomorrow for me to pick him up."

A Bad Boy Stole My Heart:
A Detroit Love Story

By: Londyn Lenz

Published by ***Miss Candice Presents***

"No Yatta! I don't know how long you're going to keep him. OUTCH!" I pulled her hair harder making her lean backwards more.

"It don't matter how fucking long I keep my son. You better have him fucking ready. I swear Cleo, if you be on some stupid shit I will pop one in yo' fuckin' head," I roughly let her go and walked out her stupid ass apartment. I don't even put my hands-on females, but Cleo talks to muthafuckin' much. I hate that I had a baby with her ass.

Every time I thought about the shit I just wanna kick my own ass. I was drunk as fuck some months back before I got locked up. Trippin' off some lean, a pill and some weed I left the club on some horny shit. I didn't feel like fucking with a new bitch so I hit Cleo rat ass up. She stayed in these apartments on Greenfield on Detroit's Westside. I popped up on her ass without calling and she had some nigga over. I threw his lame ass out and fucked her all night without a fucking condom. God wasn't with a nigga that night because some weeks later she found out she was pregnant. I denied the fuck out of the shit all the way up until she gave birth. I refused to see the baby until I found out if he was mine.

We took a DNA test the same day she had him and that shit came back 99.9% that I was the daddy. I was so fucked up I had us take another one and got the same results. I had to be a man like my uncle raised me and step up. I moved Cleo off Greenfield and into a nice two-bedroom in Dearborn, MI by Fairlane Mall. Shit was nice as fuck with high ceilings, kitchen appliances, a workout room and a pool. This ungrateful bitch didn't have to pay for shit and she still ran her fucking mouth. Her fucking rent wasn't cheap either.

Shit cost eleven-hundred a month but I paid her shit on time and all her utilities. I even got this bitch a 2016 Honda CR-V. Say what'chu wanna say about me. I wasn't getting' that rat ass bitch a 2018 nothing. The car ran good as fuck, had all the amenities and went from point A to point B. The only good thing I could say about Cleo was she gave me a cute ass son. Shit, I can't even say that because his daddy was a fine muthafucka. Anyways, since knocking her up. I ain't stuck my dick in her since. Not even when she was pregnant and you know niggas swear on pregnant pussy. That bitch could only suck my dick and only if I couldn't find another bitch to do it. Her ass would never ever, ever get this good dick again. My next child would be by my wife and I know exactly who that is.

***

"Ok, so I got word from my guys about a very exclusive auction given at the Hay-Adams hotel in Washington D.C. in a few weeks. This is a big ass hit! We looking at a hundred G's a piece and that's minimum. Havoc did his usual and later on this week he coming out here to get the shit set in motion," my uncle Lonell was talking to me and my homies while we were smoking in his basement.

Let me let y'all in about me and what the fuck I do. Well, what me and my homies were taught to do by my uncle. So, I was born to a crack head suicidal woman. The only time my mama wasn't doing drugs was when she was pregnant with me. God was looking out for a nigga because I didn't have shit in my system. When I was four-months my weak ass daddy was caught sucking him and my mama drug dealer off. She snapped and killed them niggas and then put the pistol in her fucking mouth. Leaving me alone screaming and crying for two days. Detroit police was called to sit my mama and pops out on the street. They came in the apartment on some 'get the fuck out shit' and found three dead bodies and a crying baby.

The only kin my mama had was her older brother which is my uncle Lonell and his wife Juziel. Police called them and told them the situation. Without a second thought, my uncle and his wife came and got me. I have lived with them until I got my own spot in downtown Detroit. My uncle was like my father and my auntie was like my mama. Growing up, we always had nice ass shit. Nice cars, every toy, video game system, clothes, gym shoes I wanted. We had a nice ass big house on Lancashire street. Big ass homes surrounded ours and it made the shit look nice as hell. You had some money if you lived in one of these nice ass houses. My whole life, my uncle and his best guy Havoc walked and carried themselves like some goons. Dressed down as fuck, never flashy and straight old school.

I never seen my uncle go to a nine to five. But my auntie shopped non-stop and had a new car every year. We went out of town every summer. I had whatever I wanted with my only responsibilities being house and yard work. So when I was fourteen I started asking my uncle questions. He sat me down and told me him and Havoc were thieves. My ass thought like breaking in houses and stealing from stores. He told me they go out of town and steal shit like paintings, jewelry, Persian rugs, foreign cars. My uncle and his guy Havoc either sold the items on the black market or steal it for someone for a big ass price. Even though my uncle and auntie had degrees from U of M (University of Michigan) he was still making more money than people slaving at any damn company. I knew I wanted in.

Alaric and Z have been my niggas since our sandbox days at Gardner Elementary school. So I asked my uncle if they could get down with us. He was cool with it and from then on, its been us doing this shit. I can't lie and say it wasn't fun as fuck and gives my dick a stiff. We stole from rich muthafuckas that wouldn't miss it anyway. They'd write this shit off on taxes or call their insurance company and have them handle it. We were so clean and neat with the shit. Our last ride was at L.A. Banquets in Los Angeles. There was a silent auction that Havoc found. It was all these artificial artifacts from this prince in Africa. He was selling his shit to pay off some debt or something like that. I don't know and I don't care. Anyways, they kept all the shit in the banquet for buyers to pick up. Me and Zamir dressed as janitors in the building.

We let my uncle, Havoc, and Alaric know when shit was clear. Havoc made fake identification and bank accounts for my uncle. He portrayed himself as one of the people who brought some items. While they loaded my uncle's rental truck up with the items they *believed* he brought. Me, Alaric, Zamir, and Havoc loaded our van in the back of the building up with the other shit. We didn't wipe them clean because that's to noticeable. But we took enough that we each made seventy-five grand a piece. We did about five jobs a year for a minimum of fifty grand a piece.

Shit was smooth and I had no plans on slowing down. Hell none of us did. The only rule my uncle had was all three of us had to finish school. Me and Alaric graduated from Central High school, MI in 2015. Zamir was a year older then us he graduated in 2014. We actually were all some book smart ass niggas. My auntie made sure of that shit. She used to tell me don't no real bitch want a nigga that can't read or write.

That was all I needed to hear. I made sure I had just as much book smarts as streets. My only flaw would be my crazy ass way of thinking. I hate to lose and I never ever play fucking fare. I'm selfish as fuck with my shit. I just wanna get that out the way right now so off rip, y'all know who they fuck ya reading about. I gotta keep the shit a ceno. It's the only way I know how to be. Anyways that's enough of this old shit. Now y'all know more about ya boy.

"Shit sounds good to me. Good lookin' on that lawyer Unc. He got me off and with no parole," I gave my Uncle some play.

"Money talks and bullshit walks. You know I got'chu nephew. Yo' auntie gave me hell every day you were in there. *Get my baby home!* That's all she said," we all laughed as he tried to sound like my auntie.

Thump!

"Don't be talking about me nigga! I was for real though. All of y'all my babies I don't want to see y'all behind bars or in the ground. He wasn't getting no pussy until he got you out of there," me and the homies cracked up at my auntie crazy ass. Her and my uncle been rocking since freshman year of high school. She was bad as fuck with a body like radio personality Deelishis. My auntie Juzel's face wasn't busted like that bitch though but her complexion and her height was the same. She was bad and my uncle would pop any nigga over her. Hell, he has before.

"Get'cho lying ass outta here! I was busting yo' shit down on day two of yo' so-called 'strike'," my uncle shot back. She waved him off and told us we could come eat. She made this big seafood platter with lobster tails, fried shrimp, fried catfish, Alaskan crab legs and Red lobster biscuits. She cooked like it was for a fucking party. I was happy as fuck though because my auntie could cook her ass off. I was definitely taking a to-go plate home.

"You ready to turn-up at your party tomorrow night?" Ric asked us while we all piled up our plates.

"Hell yea, nigga! I went to get some top from Cleo's ratchet' ass but she was on some dumb shit. I nutted all on her fake ass lashes. So, tomorrow night is needed. I'm bringing some bitches to the room with me," I laughed telling them the dumb ass head Cleo gave.

"Nigga you a fool! You know bitches don't play about they fuckin' lashes. Them bitches be all crooked and shit," Zamir dumb ass said. This nigga was the giant out of me and Alaric. He didn't say much except to us and his sister. And he had a permeant death stare stuck on his face.

"Fuck that hoe. Y'all know that bitch was sucking Sway's dick while I was locked up?! Hoe think I don't know. My guy told me and I told him to handle Sway. I don't give a fuck who she fucks or sucks but it was all about respect. Nigga violated in a major way," my homies and my uncle agreed.

"Cassidy told me Erin, back from New York. You need to quit playing and lock that down," Z slick ass threw that shit out there.

I haven't seen Erin's fine ass since the beginning of last year. Cutie pie was so fucking sexy the shit didn't make any sense. In my head that was the nickname, I gave her, cutie pie. Don't laugh at my corny ass but for a long, as I can remember it just fit her. She the type of fine that even other females had to admit the shit. Her skin was light caramel complexion with a smile that will knock a nigga like me out. Her hair was a little past her shoulders and it was curly as hell. Erin's eyes were a pretty ass chestnut brown that made me weak. And baby's body! Oh my God, it is so fucking bad. She was thick wit her shit! Ass nice and fat with nice titties that sit up in anything she wears. I wouldn't mind getting to know her body personally. But Erin was a good girl. She was into painting and drawing and she mastered that shit.

I used to watch her sit outside her house and she would paint for hours. She used to drive her Neon when we were in high school to certain spots in the hood and just draw. I have never seen her work for myself but I know she was passionate about the shit. Her best friend was my niggas sister so I been watching her for some time now. She the type that any nigga with sense would try his best to build with. Back in the day, I used to tell myself I wasn't that nigga because I was straight hood. I looked at cutie pie and knew she was greater then the shit around us so I just stayed away and crushed from afar. I kept rat bitches with good bodies in my face and misuse and abused they fucking asses.

I do what the fuck I want and don't give a fuck who catch feeling in the process. I been knew since the first time I laid eyes on Erin that she was something special. A Detroit goon like myself didn't need no level-headed bitch like that. Now, shit was different and all while I was locked up besides my son, I thought about her ass. I wanted Erin to be mine all fucking mine and I was going to make that shit happen one way or another. But you know how niggas is, I had to play the shit cool.

"Oh, that's what's up. I ain't seen her in a nice little minute. I ain't tryna lock that shit down though. Me and her wouldn't mix well at all. Physically yea but that would be it," Ric ugly ass laughed.

"You can front all you want nigga. You feeling her cute ass just like Z feeling her cousin Dreka. Big ass giant scares the hell out of her," me and my uncle cracked up. Z gave that nigga the middle finger. Ric wasn't lying though Z was feeling Dreka tuff as hell. He just hasn't told her. But he low key stopped niggas from getting at her. That nigga crazier than me. Dreka went to prom with Erin as her date. Not because she wasn't fine but because Z told niggas she was off limits. Them Central niggas were all scared of his big ass because of all the rumors flying around about him. But he'll fill y'all in on that.

"Nigga fuck you!" That's all Z could say making all of us laugh at how mad he was. These fools some nuts.

Erin

"Excuse me. Excuse me. Excuse me, damn," I was getting annoyed as I walked through Detroit Metropolitan Airport.

You would think I came back home during the holiday season the way it was so crowded in here. It was in the middle of May and the airport was packed as shit! I was coming from New York studio school for drawing and painting. The program was two years if you went full-time. I worked so I was part-time. After a year of being in New York, I was ready to go home. Although, I would never let go of my passion. I just wanted to be home until I figured out how I was going to have my own art studio. Drawing and painting has been a passion of mines since I was a little girl.

To be able to pick up some paper, pencil or brush and draw my feelings came so natural to me. It was apart of me and I took my art seriously. I graduated from Central High school in Detroit, MI three years ago. Central was dead smack in the hood of Detroit on Tuxedo street near Dexter area. Fights, shooting, police, canine dogs were all around my high school. Those were still some of the best four-years of my life. I didn't even live in that area but I wanted to go to the same high school my daddy and uncle graduated from. Go figure. Detroit is my city and as crazy as it is I have never been afraid of it. Disappointed would describe how I feel about my home.

Anyways, my teachers and my family wanted me to graduate and immediately go to art school. Me being a rebel I decided to go to Oakland Community College. My major was in accounting and I was going to become a tax preparer. Don't ask me why it's just what I chose. Like I said, I was rebelling against what everyone said I should do. I wasted a whole year and had a bunch of dead in jobs. My heart was still on drawing I was just afraid of putting myself out there and getting rejected. The first school of my choice was in New York and once I put my fear aside and applied I got in. I was so sad to leave home and leave my family. But I did it and feel really good about taking a chance on myself. New York was amazing, expensive as fuck! But amazing none the less!

I just missed my family and really wanted to come home. My dad got me a job working at his friend art store in Royal Oak. He sells imitations of real historic paintings from all over the world. My dad sent him my portfolio and he hired me on the spot. I could make some nice money so I jumped on that opportunity and hurried up back home. One of my first goals while home was getting my own place. My dad wouldn't have mind me staying home and living with him. But naw, I needed my own spot and my own money.

"ERINNNN!" I looked up smiling big when I saw my cousin Dreka running towards me. We crashed into each other hugging one another tight as fuck. This was my favorite cousin out of the many we had. We didn't even call each other cousins. She was my sister/cuz and from birth, me and her have been thick as thieves.

"Oh my God I have missed you boo! Come on before Uncle E thinks the worst and have the whole Detroit police looking for us," we both laughed as she picked up one of my bags and I followed her towards the car. She told me Cassidy, our best friend, had to work late so she couldn't come to pick me up with her. Dreka wasn't lying about my dad coming to look for us. I was his only child and he took over-protectiveness to an all-time high. My dad was a detective for the Detroit Police Department and sometimes in other cities to. He was that good and had a lot of clout. He's been on the force since before I was born and he loves his job. He takes pride in his job. His ass never lets me forget about his damn job. It has run plenty of boyfriends away and made me lose a lot of friends.

"Oh, my goodness bitch! Uncle D got you this new

car! I love it Dreka!" I smiled and looked at her 2018 Hyundai Sonata in awe. It was so cute and black on black just like my cousin loved.

"Thanks, boo. Yes, she is gorgeous and it was only right that I name her Midnight," we both put my bags in the trunk and got in. As soon as she started the car Beyoncé Freakum Dress song came on loud as hell. This bitch loved Beyoncé. She was a true beehive fan, you couldn't speak bad about that woman to Dreka. She turned it down and pulled a blunt from her sun visor.

"Yo' ass stay playing this damn girl. Not right now bitch, turn to 107.9," I said as I went to the FM radio station. The Breakfast Club was on and I knew we were in for some laughs.

Dreka lit her blunt and took a few puffs. Passing it to me I took some as we hotboxed it to the freeway. I missed my city so much. People talk shit about Detroit but it was my home and if you've never been here then shut the fuck up. It can do a lot better but tell me a city or town that's perfect. I was happy as fuck to be home. The first thing that popped in my head was the Riverwalk downtown. I get such inspiration for my drawings when I sit by the water and let my mind be free. I love drawing or painting what's around me minus the people.

I never ever draw people and I'll elaborate on that later. Dreka was speeding fast as fuck down seven-mile and Livernois like she wanted to end our lives. Thank God I was a little high. I smiled looking at all the big houses in our neighborhood. When me and Dreka were little we used to call them castles. Any homes in the 48221-zip code was usually spacious and more than three bedrooms. I knew we weren't going to my daddy's house because our grandma would have a fit if I didn't see her first. Grandma stayed with Dreka and her dad, my uncle D. I saw Dreka make a phone call before she turned down Fairfield street. Looking out the window I saw my daddy outside smiling. Along with a red 2018 Kia Stinger and a big white bow on top of it. I looked at

Dreka with a big ass Kool-Aid smile and she smiled big as fuck back and said.

"Bitch you know my Uncle was not about to let you come home with no wheels. Me and Cassidy picked it out along with the color. I call her 'Cherry Bomb'," I smiled and hugged her as we both hopped out.

"OH, MY GOODNESS DADDYYYYY! I LOVE IT! I LOVE IT! I LOVE ITTTT! Thank you!" I hugged him tight again and ran to my new car. She was beautiful and I understood why Dreka named her Cherry bomb. I opened the door and inhaled the new car smell. My daddy and Dreka were cheesing from the outside. I rolled the windows up and down. I swear I had the best daddy in the world. My grandma did good raising him and my uncle D. After I enjoyed the car we all went in the house.

"My Muse! Your daddy has missed you!" I smiled and gave my daddy a big ass hug. I have missed him so much and missed him calling me my nickname. He gave me the name 'muse' because he put the paintbrush and pencil in my hand when I was small. Him and my mama used to paint all the time but when I came along they had to focus more on money then their passion. I believe that's why me and my mama's relationship is so estranged now. She blames me for taking my father from her and for stopping them from living their care-free lives. Like I made her spread her legs and pop her pussy for my daddy.

"I missed you more daddy. You seem taller and please cut some of this beard daddy," I looked at him laughing and shaking my head. My dad was about 6'4, tall and slim with a bald head and a long ass sandy brown beard. I mean it's so long that it could be flat-ironed and look like a bundle of hair. He was light as hell just like my ass with light brown eyes. All my friends used to come over just to stare at my dad. Ugh!

"These women out here love your daddy beard my muse. So, did Dreka drive you here safely? I know she drives fast just like my baby brother," he joked while hugging

Dreka and kissing her on top of her head. Dreka was close to my dad just like I was close to hers. I loved my uncle Delon.

"Uncle E don't be talking about me. But we did blaze up in the car while on the freeway," Dreka always calls my dad uncle E, which was short for Emmanuel. I shot my cousin a crazy ass look as she cracked up. My dad looked at both of us and shook his head.

"I know damn well you ain't buying weed from people you don't know. What if that shits laced Erin? Only cop from me and you know that," I gave him my sad face that I knew always gets him. Yea my dad was the police but he um, let's just say sometimes he bent the rules. Just a little though never much. He was my hero and made it his business to get the scum bags out of Detroit. My whole life he has taught me the difference between good and bad.

"I don't mean to trip on y'all but people shady as hell these days. And Dreka you can bets believe I will be letting yo' daddy know this shit too," I stuck my tongue out at her and she started pouting.

"My grandbaby. Look at you!" I looked up at my grandma as she walked up the stairs from the basement. I hugged my grandma tight and kissed her cheeks. She smelled like peppermint. Her long snow-white hair was in a big braid hanging down her back and stopping at her butt. I missed my family so much.

"New York ain't been feeding you, sweetie? Grandma got you. I got some turkey legs, cornbread, macaroni and cheese, and greens. Emmanuel, get off your ass and get this meat out the oven. Lazy ass nigga," me and Dreka cracked up along with my daddy.

"Damn ma why I gotta be a lazy nigga?! And why you cook all this food like it's a holiday?" As soon as my dad set the pan on the stove my grandma hit him with her oven mitten.

"I haven't had both my grandbaby's together in a year. It is a damn holiday, now go wash up so we can all eat," we all washed our hands as my grandma set the table up.

"So, that annoying ass ex-wife of yours couldn't come to greet her only child after being gone for a year?" My grandma looked at my father and asked referring to my mama. Me and Dreka hit each other's leg under the table. My grandma couldn't stand my mama with a passion.

"Ma, fuck Josey a'ight. I told her that Erin was coming home and she gave me a million excuses as to why she couldn't make it," my dad responded as he looked over at me and smiled. I knew later he would be giving me an extra hug and some money. He always felt bad for how my mama did me. He has put his foot up her ass plenty of times for mistreating me but she just doesn't change.

"But she was there every step of the way for her ugly ass son she had on you. Swear I can't stand that jezebel bitch," when my grandma said that me and Dreka almost spit our lemonade out. My dad shook his head laughing. My Josey Monroe aka my mama cheated on my father when I was two-years-old. She claimed my dad loved me more than her. So she cheated, he beat the guy and my mama up and put my her out. Now she lives in Lansing with her son and husband. Who by the way is two years older than me and she raised to hate me and my dad's guts. I have never even met him or his dad. The only thing I knew was his name and he was studying to be a lawyer. It was something my maam brought up to me anytime she did decide to see or talk to me.

"Damn, so y'all gone eat in my house without me! And look at my favorite niece blossoming out!" I jumped up from the table and hugged my uncle Delon as he came in. His ass was just as big as my daddy and equally handsome. He hugged me, Dreka and my grandma. Giving my dad some play he sat down next to Dreka. We all laughed, ate good food and cracked jokes.

"You riding with me to see Cassidy right?" Dreka asked as she put her gold flip-flops on. Swear my cousin was the prettiest plus size girl ever. I wouldn't even consider her plus size because she had shape.

"Girl you know I'm going with you to see my boo. My dad is not happy about it but I told him I would spend all tomorrow with him," Dreka put her long black maxi dress on and put her long curly bundles in a ponytail. Bitch hair was longer than mine and she still wore weave. I had on a floral crochet romper that fell off the shoulders. A pair of silver strappy sandals and my hair in its natural curly state which fell a little pass my shoulders. Dreka grabbed her purse, we said goodbye to our family and we headed to Cassidy's house.

***

"AHHHHHH!" Me and Cassidy screamed in unison when she opened her apartment door. Hugging her tight I was smiling from ear to ear! I think I missed her and Dreka the most. We both met Cassidy freshman year in high school. Her big ass brother was fucking some nigga up in the hallway. He went all *Staci* from the movie *The Wood* on him because he slapped her on the ass. Dreka thought the shit was funny as hell and the rest was history.

"Oh, my goodness bitch I have missed you. Yo' ass bet not ever leave me again with this nutty hoe," Cassidy joked pointing to Dreka.

"Bitch don't come for me. You love me and you know it!" Dreka joked as we all plopped down on the couch.

"So, how was New York? Was it like television made it?" Cassidy was cheesing and waiting for me to answer.

"Bitch we talked to her every day!" Dreka threw Cassidy's throw pillow at her. I laughed listening to them play argue. I missed them both so much and honestly. If they were with me in New York I would have stayed.

"Oh, my goodness y'all argue like y'all married. Cass, New York was amazing. It was crowded and expensive as fuck. But it's a place that as I get older I would consider living. I got so many paintings and drawings from the Apple city. Very inspirational. Now! Can we talk about something else? Like how we are going to turn up for my return home!" Laughing I grabbed some chips that Cassidy must have been eating on.

"Oook, well here's a change of subject. Yatta was released from jail yesterday," Cassidy had this stupid grin on her face. Looking to the left of me so did Dreka.

"Why do I care," both of these hoes sighed loud as hell and smacked their crusty ass lips.

"Hoe pleaseee stop faking for the gram! You like him, he likes you and y'all been doing this dance since freshman year," Cassidy said while Dreka perched her lips together and nodding her head.

"You and him are almost as bad as this bitch and my brother," she was pointing to Dreka when she said that. Her stupid ass was caught off guard by Cassidy's comment.

"Bitch what the hell does that mean? Me and Z don't have shit going on-----," Cassidy cut her off just like she did me.

"Dreka chill on the lies. Y'all may not have shit going on but you like him. And you must have put a spell on his ass because he never likes a bitch. But he is all in a trance when he's around you. Whyyy do you and Erin wanna keep up these shenanigans?" When she yelled that last part I smacked my lips and waved her off.

"Wait a hot damn minute! What about you and Ric?! When you finally give up that gush between your legs then you can come at us!" Dreka jumped up and yelled

"YAS COUSIN!" Giving me a high five and falling back on the couch laughing. Cassidy turned her nose up, waved us off as she got up and walked into her kitchen.

"Naw bitch don't run!" me and Dreka were about to get up and tease her some more. But someone knocked on her door. Cassidy walked out her kitchen but not before sticking her tongue out at us. When she looked through her peephole to see who it was she turned and looked with the biggest smile on her face. As soon as she opened the door I understood.

"Hey my favorite and only big brother, come on in," she hugged Z closing the door behind him. I looked at my cousin out the side of my eye. Her whole posture changed and her leg started shaking. Now, even though me her and Cassidy are mad close. Me and Dreka are family so we knew all intimate shit about one another. I been knew she was into Z. Hell, if you ask me she sounds in love the way she talks about his huge ass. And looking at her now, this bitch couldn't hide it if she tried.

"What's good Cassy," calling Cassidy by the nickname he gave her Z hugged and kissed her on top of her head. Walking all the way end he looked at me shocked and said.

"What up doe Miss. New York! How fucking ironic is it that you came home the same time my boy did," I hugged him and rolled my eyes at his comment. I was tired of him and his sister slick ass remarks about me and Yatta. Hell, there is no me and Yatta. He has a whole damn family and even if he didn't----- Oh God listen to me rambling! I do that shit when I'm nervous, not that I'm nervous I just----- never mind back to the story.

"What up doe Dreka, how you doin' girl?" Me and Cassidy looked at Z's face when he spoke to Dreka. He had a small smirk and his eyes were squinted.

"I been good Z. How you?" her ass was trying hard not to smile.

"What I tell you about that Z shit?" He gave her a hug and looked down at her. Nigga was a full giant. Dreka's cheeks got flushed, she twirled the end of her hair and smiled.

"My bad *Zamir,* I been good how are you?" me and Cassidy looked at each other with big smiles and our mouths open. Now, how the fuck could both of them even front like they not feeling each other.

"UMMM! What are you doing poppin' up at my crib?" Cassidy's loud mouth broke their fucking trance. He looked at her and shook his head.

"Cassy, I'm not dealing with *your mama* by myself. If it was up to me it would be fuck her all around," his face changed instantly from soft when looking at Dreka. To hard and scary as fuck when he talked about him and Cassidy's mama. We all knew their relationship was estranged. Nobody knew why though.

"Oh shit, I'm sorry boos. I forgot I gotta ride with Z. But we on for tomorrow night right?" Cassidy looked at me and Dreka. I saw my cousin look at Cassidy like she fucked up. Z dropped his head and shook it. I looked at all three of them with a confused face.

"Why y'all looking dumb?" When I asked that Dreka was pulling my arm out of Cassidy's apartment. Cassidy was looking like she pissed on herself.

"Ok y'all we will holla later," Dreka yelled as she opened the door and pulled me out.

"Dreka what the hell was that about?" My eyebrows were furrowed, and she laughed and pulled her cell phone out.

"Nothing boo, we were going to surprise you with a night out. Cassidy's big ass mouth was supposed to stay shut," we were in her car and she was texting on her phone while she talked. I know this hoe like the back of my hand. I knew when she lied, she couldn't look at you without laughing. I looked at her ass for a minute and decided to let it go. Putting my seat belt on I just hoped these fuckers known as my cousin and best friend weren't up to shit sneaky.

Cassidy

"Yo' mouth from the south ass," Z shook his head as we got in his white Ford 2018 Expedition. My big ass brother only looked right in trucks.

"I knowwww! My God why can't my pretty ass mouth just stay closed! Dreka texted me cussing me out," I laughed and held my phone up to show Z. He looked from the road at my phone shaking my head. I lived in Dearbornat the Fairlane Woods apartments and our mom lived on Turner Street on the west side. Straight hood shit. Z fast driving ass took Greenfield-Street like the police won't pull his ass over. You ever drive with someone who drives crazy but never gets a ticket? But the minute you do a little speed you get pulled over?! Shit grinds my fucking gears!

"I'm telling yo' ass right now Cassy. If your mama start that shit I swear the next visit, You on your fuckin' own," he looked at me with a serious expression once he got to a red light.

Since I was little Zamir and our mother never got along. I can remember as far back to when I was four-years-old. Zamir is only a year older than me and we were in his room. My big brother always wanted me close to him when we were at home. If we weren't at home he always wanted to know where I was and who I was with. He has just always been protective of me. I love him for that but sometimes I think it stops him from living. Anyways, I was sitting on Z's bed playing with my baby doll. He was on his floor playing with his wrestling men. My mom was arguing with her newest boyfriend for that week. I hated all the screaming and crying so instantly I started to cry.

Z got up and consoled me. He told me that everything was going to be ok. He would give me his headphones and let me watch my Nick Jr. DVD on my portable DVD player.

Growing up, I always had more toys and electronics than Z. But, I was a girl so I guess I was more high maintenance then he was. While I watched TV and Z went back to playing his bedroom door flung open. My mama would start yelling and cussing at us. Making me start crying again, and Z having to calm me down. Our mama would yell at Z and tell him to shut me up. She would yell, cuss and then go get drunk as fuck all day. Our mother had been drinking since before we were born. She would go out at night and a new nigga would be at our breakfast table in the morning.

That was our childhood all the way until Z got his own place at eighteen. Of course, he had me come live with him. At first, my mama objected and even threaten to call the police on him because I was only seventeen. But, all he did was buy her a bottle of Seagram's Gin and all was forgotten. I loved living with my brother. There was no arguing, fighting and me and him got along so good. Yatta and Ric started coming over and even then, Z still made sure they acted appropriately when I was around. They never had girls over but then again Z was so fucking mean and anti-social I didn't even expect to see girls around his apartment.

And to make shit so crazy, girls loved his big scary ass. But I owe so much to my brother and would fuck a bitch up if she did him wrong. That's why I wanted him and Dreka to stop playing and just get together. I have a feeling that she would be good for his hard ass. She would just have her hands full with breaking down that tough exterior he has up. Turning down Eaton and Turner street I looked at how bad our childhood block looked.

I mean, the hood is the hood but it used to not look so abandoned. Homes that used to have people living in them were now boarded up or sat on fire. Some were knocked over and just left a vacant lot. It's a shame because I can remember running up and down my street. Neighbors telling my mama where I was and all the kids running outside when we heard the ice cream truck. Shit was just depressing as fuck now when we came to visit our mama. Z parked in the beat-up drive-way and we both got out.

"What's up doe Z and Cassidy!" Marlon across the street yelled from his porch. His annoying ass was still living at home. I used to like him but Z put an end to that shit. I'm glad he did too because Marlon had six kids with five different women. I could have easily been one of them. I looked up at him and waved. Z's mean ass didn't say shit he just kept walking.

"Ma! Ma its Cassidy and Z!" I yelled as soon as we walked in her house.

It was eighty degrees outside. Mama had all the windows closed and no fans on. Her black and green furniture was still the same from when we were kids. I offered to buy her some new pieces, but she didn't want me too. Z went to the kitchen, grabbed a bottle of water and sat down at the kitchen table. I made a note to get mama's carpet cleaned. I had on a long purple maxi dress and some black BEBE flip-flops. You couldn't pay me to put my feet on mama's carpet. Walking to the back by her room I almost jumped out my skin with the sight in front of me.

"MA! Come on damn!" I pulled her bedroom door closed and went back in the dining room with Z.

"That's yo' nasty ass mama," his sarcastic ass said while drinking his water. Her bedroom door opened and the nigga whose dick she was sucking came out. He was fixing his shorts while on his phone. He got to Z and nodded his head before he walked out.

"Um, you know him Z? He looks about our age?" I asked him with dismay written all over my face.

"Yea, that's my mans, Luke. He works for me and Yatta on some private shit," he said the shit like it was no big deal that his homeboy wasn't just getting *our mama* to top him off.

"What the fuck y'all doing here fucking up my dick appointment?" Mama came from the back . She was pulling up her blue t-shirt over her head. You couldn't deny mama's beauty. Me and her were the same height,light skin with hazel eyes. Her body was nice but I was thicker than she was. Mama was slim with a toned frame but all the drinking gave her some discoloration under her eyes.

"Ma, I don't wanna hear that from you. We just came by to check on you and make sure you didn't need anything," I said as she hugged me. All I could smell was Seagram's gin and lilac body spray. She always sprayed that like it was going to drown the liquor smell out.

"Well, why the fuck you always walking around with big ass dummy for?" I inhaled in and out when she talked about Z. I knew she was going to start this shit I was just hoping Z could ignore it.

"Trust me, I didn't wanna come but it makes her happy so shut the fuck up," Z's voice was as hard and as big as he is. Could you imagine if he yelled at you? I would probably run and hide.
"Why the fuck you always doing what the fuck she says like you fucking her?"

"MA!" I yelled at her stupid ass. She had a smirk on her face while she stared at Z waiting for him to answer.

"I'm just saying. I got niggas who I fuck and suck on a daily that don't bend over backwards for me like he does for you. Anyways, have you talked to you trifling ass daddy?" she walked to the kitchen and asked me. I looked at Z with sad eyes and I swear the look he had on his face looked like all things evil. I got up and gave my big brother a hug and nudged his big head. He softened up and gave me a closed mouth smile. That was the most you would ever see Zamir smile. Or a low ass chuckle.

"Yea I talked to him this morning ma. He um, he is getting married in two months," I didn't look at my mama when I said that.

I didn't know how the hell she would take the news of daddy getting married. He isn't the best but he was consistent in my life. To be fair my mama was seventeen when she had me. My fucking daddy was only thirteen! Yea, you read the shit right. He was a thirteen-year-old hot-headed drug dealer running the streets of Detroit with his father. My mama used to fuck his dad and one day he wanted his son to get some pussy. My mama laid down and took my daddy virginity and got knocked up. The shit is the most bizarre shit I ever fucking heard. Anyways, my mama can't stand my daddy. I even think she hates him by the way she talks about him.

My daddy's father who by the way is Zamir's daddy is who mama loves. But his pimp ass wants nothing to do with her. This shit was all fucked up in my family but thank God out of all of the bullshit. Me and my brother remained close and grew-up to be normal. Well, as normal as we can be based on the situation.

"I don't give a fuck about that nigga getting married! He probably raped her and made her marry him like he did me," she yelled from the kitchen. That's another thing, mama swore my daddy raped her. She always told me I was the product of a rape but she loved me still. My daddy been sat me down and told me the story between him and my mama. For some reason, I believed him. Mama has a way of playing the victim.

"Ain't nobody rape yo' ass. You just pop that shit for any nigga that walks by and then get mad when a nigga rejects you," I popped my head up at Zamir and his remark. I knew that was all it took for my mama to pop off.

"Shut'cho stupid ass up! That nigga did rape me and your fucking father didn't do shit about it! What the fuck do you know wit'cho country lookin' ass!" her words were slurred as she tried to come towards Z. I jumped up and as soon as I did that she slapped the fuck out of me. I think I feared more for her than for my light skin face.

"THA FUCK!" Z leaped up from his seat and pushed mama to the floor. It didn't take much for her to fall over. As big as Z is, I knew he didn't use all his strength.

"Bitch is you crazy puttin' yo' fuckin' dry ass hands on my sister!" he yelled at her and turned to me. My face was stinging and I could taste a little blood from my lip. My mama started laughing as tears fell from my face.

"Help mama up Cassidy and quit being dramatic," she had the nerve to hold her hand out for me to help her up. Z pulled me behind him, picked up her Seagram's gin bottle and threw it against the wall making it shatter.

"Aw you done did it now you big retarded bitch! I swear when I get up I'm fuckin' yo' giant ass up!" she tried to get up but was too drunk to find her balance. Z smacked his lips and waved her off. He grabbed my hand and we walked out her house. She was calling him all kinds of fucked up ass names. To make it so bad. Zamir was smart as fuck! He was the one who used to tutor me all through middle and high school. Mama knew it but she still called him stupid and dumb because of his size.

"Cassy, you know I love you baby sis. But I'm not coming back here unless we cleaning out the house after she is dead. And probably not even then so don't ask," his deep ass voice had no inch of humor in it.

"Ok Z I understand. I'm sorry for even making you come. I just wish you and mama can get y'all shit together," he passed me some tissues from his glove compartment. Wiping my face and lip Z said.

"Ain't gone ever happen Cassy so stop pressing. Come on, I'm taking you to get something to eat then I gotta make some moves. Ima leave you with some hundreds so you can go shopping for Yatta's party tomorrow night," I smiled at him and nodded my head. My big brother was so sweet. I just wish I knew what was the deal with him and mama. The way my brother loved me, I knew he would make a woman happy as fuck one day. He just had to open his heart and stop being so hard. Hopefully, my best friend can break his ass down.

***

Knock!
Knock!
Walking to my door I looked at my phone in my hand and saw I fell asleep for about an hour. It was a little after

four o' clock in the afternoon. After dealing with mama crazy ass me and Z went to White Castle's to eat and then he dropped me off. Like he said he was going to do. He gave me five-hundred dollars for me to go shopping. I came home, showered, threw on my Elmo pajama shorts and cami. Before I knew it I was passed out sleep in my Queen-size bed. Looking through the peephole. I smiled when I saw Alaric standing at the door. I was like a little school girl whenever I was around him. I told him to hold on while I ran to the bathroom. Shit, I had just woken up so I know I was looking a little busted. Lawd!

Alaric (Ric)

I chuckled when Cassidy's sweet voice told me to hold on. I had popped up on her little ass so I knew she was trying to make sure she was on her game before letting me in. I don't know why the fuck she thought she had to do that for a nigga. Cassidy was already fine as fuck with her slim thick ass. How fucking crazy is it that I would be into my nigga's baby sister? But this shit was bound to happen. I had been feeling Cassidy since we were in high school. Even though I kept my shit on the low I still knew eventually I was gonna get at her. When we were little I never even looked twice at Cassidy in that light.

Call a nigga vain but she was quiet and innocent. She used to love clothes that were too fucking big for her. That face was always bad as fuck but my ass thought she was a dyke. Not saying I wouldn't have turned her ass out. But that was the homies little sister so I hurried and pushed it out my head. Senior year in high school is when I started looking at her in a different fucking light. Dreka and Erin pulled her quiet ass out her shell and made her take notice of her looks and body. Well, the shit caught my muthafuckin' eye and I sat out to make lil mama mine.

My only problem was letting my nigga know what was up. I ain't got an'ounce of bitch in me. But I know how much Z loves his sister. Me, him and Yatta have done some damage to these bitches. We done exposed hoes, ran trains, recorded and straight ran through these hoes. Not giving a fuck what they thought or felt. And before y'all turn ya noses up at us everything we did with bitches was consensual. My point is the nigga know how much of a dog I am. Hell, we all are. I'm not saying a nigga was a changed man but I wasn't going to be as ruthless with Cassidy as I was with other bitches. Two months ago I popped up at her job in Fairlane mall. I told her I needed to holla at her when she got off. We exchanged numbers and I came over her crib and chilled that same night.

I told her cute ass that I was feeling her and wanted to fuck with her. Her light bright ass turned red and said we could see where shit goes. Now, I'm still a nigga so I didn't let all my hoes go that day. As of right now, I got a couple of hoes, hell I was a fine fucking nigga. I just wanted to see what was up with lil mama and give the shit my all the best way I could. Shit at twenty-one-years-old I had no idea if I was ready to settle down. But I had been in relationships before, well in situationships. Although I cheated on every single last one of them. I still knew how to treat a woman. And I knew as of right now I don't want Cassidy talking to anybody else. I just needed to tell my nigga Z what was up. I heard her door unlock and she opened it smiling

"About fucking time-----," my sentence was cut short when I seen her face. That's what made me pop up. Z caught up with me and Yatta so we could handle some business. We got the drop about this quick hit in Grand Haven. We looking at a quick fifty grand a piece. Havoc found out last minute and since none of us turned down money, we hopped on it. While we were meeting up Z told us about him and Cassidy going to visit their drunk ass mama. After he told us I made it my business to come check on my Cass love.

"It doesn't hurt Ric," she gave me a half smile when I touched the side of her face. She had a cut on the side of her lip. Because Cass skin was so light you could see the print of her mama's hand on the side of her face. My nostrils flared and I swear if it was any other bitch I would fuck them up. Hell, if she told me right now to do something I would.

"Cass love you gotta chill on your mama for a minute. She ain't fucking well and it's only a matter of time before she does some fucking damage to you. Z ain't gone have to kill her ass because I will gladly do the shit first," I walked in her apartment.

The minute she closed the door and locked it I picked her short ass up. Cassidy was 5'0 even and I was 6'2. My complexion was a shade darker than hers. As soon as I picked her up them nice ass thighs and legs wrapped around my waist. My Detroit Pistons Grant Hill jersey had my arms on display for her to grab. I had her back pressed against the door and my hands squeezing her round booty. Me and Cassidy still were figuring our thing out but we did smash on a regular. This shit was new for me but I just knew that I didn't want her fucking around with anybody else. So, I'll play the part she needed me to play.

"You know I will gladly fuck yo' mama up for you. Just for her fucking up this beautiful face, whatever you need Cass," I was dead ass about that shit. Her mama been hell in Cassidy's and Zamir's life since day one.

"It's fine Ric. For real let's just forget about it. I take it Z told you and Yatta what happened?" I nodded my head yea. Cassidy reached in the back of my head and pulled my rubber band off my dreads. When she did that I knew she wanted some dick. My dreads were always on point and they touched the middle of my back. Swear that shit made Cassidy's pussy wet because she was always making them hang.

"I texted you last night and you never responded. So, that's how we doing?" I smacked my lips at her ass.

"Chill out with that shit Cassidy. A nigga was busy getting' his bread right wasn't nobody ignoring yo' ass," I looked towards her kitchen because it smelled good as hell in her apartment.

"What'chu cook? I'm hungry as hell."

"I made some chicken tacos, you can help yourself," she was saying that but her hands were still in my dreads.

"Naw, it can wait," I licked my lips and leaned forward to kiss her.

Cassidy had some nice pouty ass lips that were soft as hell. Her breath was always on point and her grill was the shit. I have been in situations where a bitch breath would smell like a donkey's ass. Those hoes I wouldn't even let lick my big toe. Cassidy however, her shit was always fresh. Ma also was the first chick I talked to with a short haircut. Like she had her shit chopped off all around her head with some long hair left at the front. The shit would fall down over her left eye making it sexy as hell. I never talked to a bald head bitch before.

Shit just wasn't my thing. But Cassidy ass made the shit rock and fit just for her. Plus, her grade of hair was cute as fuck so it looked nice. I let my tongue into her mouth and that's when shit got heated. Cassidy started grinding her body into mine while I still held her up. I gripped her tighter and started moving towards her couch. Once I reached it I pulled away from our kiss and let her down.

"Let me see you strip," I said to her as I took my shoes, socks, and shirt off.

Now, my dick game is the shit but fucking with Cassidy. I like to give her control because she was so sweet. Her little innocent ass had some freak in her. Shit was sexy as fuck watching her come out of her shell. I sat down on the couch and watched her do her thang. She didn't have much to take off. Pulling her tank top over her head she had a black see-through bra on. Her caramel nipples were showing. Shit was cute as fuck because she was shy with it but still continued. I licked my lips when she took her shorts off and had matching see-through panties on. Cassidy's body was the fucking shit.

Tiny ass waist with some nice size thighs and a perfectly shaped ass that was round and soft. She stepped out her house shoes and showed them pretty ass feet. Another plus for me! It was so many bitches in Detroit that walked around with their feet lookin' like they took a hammer to them bitches. Cassidy's feet was small and always polished like her nails. A bright ass pink was what she rocked today and I couldn't wait to have them bitches in the air. I watched her take her bra off and slide her panties down.

That nice pussy was bald with one thin line of hair

down the middle. My fucking dick was turning all the way up in my damn shorts. Her titties were a perfect C-cup and round as hell just wanting me to play with them. Cassidy walked her fine naked ass over to me and started undoing my shorts. I raised up a little and helped her pull them down along with my boxers. My shit was nine-inches and thick as fuck. As soon as Cassidy straddled me she went back to giving me kisses. I broke that shit and started licking and sucking on her neck. This fuckin' girl skin was soft as hell. I never understood how bitches skin was so soft and smooth. I went from her neck on down to them round ass titties. That was Cassidy's spot.

"Oooo Ric babe. Mmm," her ass was pushing her titties further in my mouth. I was biting and pulling on her nipples. On God, I could feel my fucking lap soaking wet from her pussy. After putting some hickeys on her titties I sat back on the couch.

"Put that shit in," I told her while licking my lips at her sexy ass body. Cassidy pretty ass hands grabbed my swollen nine-inch. My shit was thick as fuck and her little hand could never fit around it. And her mouth wasn't wide enough to swallow it whole but that didn't stop her from giving some good ass dome. But we gone have to get into that another time. Right now, I need some of her pussy. Biting her bottom lip, she leaned forward a little and slip my dick into home base. My bitch ass was almost about to moan out loud! Her pussy was so fucking tight and wet. The grip that muthafucka had fucked my head all up. I folded both of my hands behind my head while laying back.

"Gone head and get loose on that dick Cass. I want'chu to squirt all on this dick," what I say that shit for? She gave me a hit ass smirk and worked that pussy so good on this dick I almost moved my ass in her crib.

"Oh, fuck Ricccc. Sss damn," Cassidy had her hands flat on the couch while leaning back. Her pretty ass titties were bouncing as she did her thang. Shit felt good as fuck but I wasn't anywhere near ready to nut.

"I'm about to cum babe. Shit!" She stopped riding and lifted up while squirting all on my dick. That shit was live as fuck. While she was squirting I yanked her little ass up by her thighs and sat her on my face. Pussy all on my mouth. I had her juices all on my lap, chest and now face. I have eaten my share of pussy but Cassidy's shit was flavorful as fuck. Hands down the fucking best.

"Fuckkkkkkk Ric! Oh, my Gosh babe!" I had my nails deep in her ass cheeks so she wouldn't move. Still eating that pussy dry I stood up with her in the air. Laying her on the couch with me still going at it. I had her back flat on the couch and her ass in the air. I was on my knees on her couch just having a feast on her pussy. Shit was sweet as fuck.

"I-I'm cummin' shitttt!" when she said that I released her clit out my mouth and started rubbing that bitch hard with my thumb.

She squirted in my mouth and on mychest. I lowered her down and slid my dick in her. My fucking face was dripping wet with her juices but I gave no fucks. My young ass was a freak. Plus, I was taking advantage of Cassidy ass not bitching about a condom. Maybe she was just caught up in the moment. Whatever it was I was going to enjoy it. A nigga didn't want any kids but I had been wanting to feel Cassidy without a rubber since she let me hit two months ago. The shit was everything I imagined it to be too. I fucked Cassidy for a good two-hours making her squirt all on her brown leather couch. After we out fucked each other we took a shower, ate and watched a movie together until it was time for me to go. I had to go see my old lady.

***

"LARIC!" My baby brother Lee ran to me as soon as I opened the front door to my mama's house. Once I started getting some real money I moved my mama and three baby brothers off of Cherrylawn and Lyndon on Detroit's west side. It was getting to fucking bad over there and I will lose it if something happens to my family. So last year I got them a house in Southfield on Filmore street. Closer to my mama's job and my little brother's school.

"What up doe lil nigga. Where mama at?" I asked him as I picked him up and tickled his bad ass.

When I got my mama the house I put some furniture in it to. Some nice shit I knew she would like from Art Van. The one thing my mama didn't play about was her furniture. When I was little I would get my ass beat if I fucked our shit up. Lee said mama was in the backyard as I put him down. He was the youngest at four-years-old. Next was Marcus who was six and June who was seven years old. Yea, my mama a little hot pussy ass but hey. That's ma dukes for ya. Four boys total and four baby daddy's total. Three of them ain't shit and don't give a fuck about their child.

My dad was the only one who gave a damn and stayed in my life. That nigga fifty-five-years old and still that fuckin' nigga with his young ass twenty-one-year-old wife. That nigga was a true ladies man and passed that shit down to me. Him and my mama couldn't stand each other but it didn't stop his ass from being around. Speaking of my dad I need to holla at that old nigga in a few days. Before I headed to the backyard I stopped in June's room.

"What up punk, what'chu in here watching man!" I hurried up and turned his DVD player off.

"Um, Anthony gave me his brother movie about boobies. I just wanted to see what they looked like." I was laughing as I took the DVD out the player.

"Look youngin' you only seven-years-old. Shit like this you don't need to focus on. Ya, hear me? School and your brothers is all you should be on until you get older. I'm out the crib so you the man. You can get pussy later on down the line. A'ight?" I told his ass. He nodded and agreed before he turned his nose up.

"What's pussy?" I laughed my ass off when he asked that.

"Aye yo', just do what I said ok? School and your brothers," I laughed and shook my head as I walked out his room. Little nigga was only seven-years-old and asking about boobies and fucking pussy. I feel like smacking my damn mama. Walking past Marcus room I saw that he was sleep while watching SpongeBob.

"Old lady, why you in the backyard but got the front door unlocked? You wanna get murdered?" I asked her as I walked down the steps to her. She was taking some ribs off the grill. It was around six o'clock in the evening.

"Boy shut up and come help me take this meat in the house," I laughed and picked up the pan of meat. I kissed her on the forehead and we both walked in the house.

"How you doin' mama?" we walked in the kitchen and I put the meat on top of the stove. The house I got her was a five-bedroom two-story home. The fifth bedroom was upstairs but she made it into a den.

"I been ok, listen I need a favor. I got a date Sunday night. Keep your brothers for me please," I looked at her with furrowed brows.

"Ma, what old ass slave looking nigga you going out with now? I swear if this nigga think he about to be living here I will burn this house down," let me explain some shit. My mama not only fucks with old niggas. She gets the ones who don't ever have shit but old balls to give her. Her ass lucked up and snagged my dad but that nigga is and will always be a player. So, when I was two my mama took me and bounced. My dad never being one to chase let her leave. Swear when y'all meet this nigga y'all gone love him.

"Boy first off don't be talking about the niggas I fuck with. Be lucky I am a little charitable because yo' ass wouldn't be here," she slapped me in the back of my head making me and her laugh. I loved the fuck out of my mama. She was wild as hell but she took care of me and my brothers good as hell. This was my best friend right here.

"You know I got yo' thot ass. I'll be here around this time," she smiled and put a plate in front of me. I watched her fix my brothers plate and set them up at the table. My mama was a good woman. Pretty as hell with my

complexion, long ass sandy brown hair and a little on the
heavy side. Her face was pretty and she had shape to her
which annoyed me because that's what made her keep being
fast. Naw, I love the fuck out of my wild ass mama.

"Ma, you know June was watching a Girls Gone Wild
DVD he got from his ugly ass friends. You need to watch
that little nigga," I told her while she poured them some
Ohana fruit punch. She popped him on his arm and said she
was calling Anthony's mama.

"Alaric why don't you invite that pretty ass Cassidy
over here when you babysit," I looked up from my plate to
see my mamas face. She had a smirk on her face as she took
a bite of her greens. My mama could throw down cooking.

"You tryna be funny old lady. I just left from chillin'
with her ma. She good where she at," taking a bite of my
ribs, my mama turned her nose up.

"You need to stop trying to be like your daddy boy.
That girl is beautiful, sweet, respectful and smart. You so
fuckin' dumb that yo ass would let that good shit pass you.
Nigga this Detroit, the hoodrats are taking over," she laughed
at her own joke.

"Cassidy is a rare joint. But nooooo, you wanna listen
to German stupid ass," I didn't even argue with her. That shit
takes to much energy. Instead, I just laughed and shook my
head while eating her good ass cooking. My mama didn't
mean any harm, she just wanted me to grab a good woman. I
just didn't tell her that I already did.

***

"What the fuck Alaric! Why is your dick still soft!"
Newbie's loud mouth ass was yelling all in my fucking face.
I was sitting in her basement and she pulled my dick out
trying to suck it. That muthafucka just wasn't waking up for
her ass. Hell, I don't even know why I came over to her crib.
After eating dinner at my mama's house. I was playing the
game with June and she called my phone. I ain't have shit up
so I figured why not. Now here I am bored, annoyed and with
a soft dick.

"Shit bitch I don't know. Maybe yo' breath hot as fuck and making my dick scared. Get the fuck up and move!" I told her funky ass while she laid between my legs. I fixed my jeans and went back to smoking my weed. Newbie lived on Northlawn by Mumford High School. I only fucked with westside bitches unless they lived downtown and that's only because that's where I lived. My crib was never an option for any bitch. Cassidy has never even been to my shit. My dad always told me you never let no bitch know where you lay your head. They'll try and move in on yo' ass when you not looking. Hell tuh tha naw! Not me!

"Fuck that shit you talking nigga. Who the fuck you been fuckin'?" When she asked that I just laughed. Newbie was cool and I had been smashing her for about four months. But she was an easy lay. She lived with her auntie who dances at Ace of Spades strip club along with this bitch named Tia who Z fucked with. All I did with Newbie was smoke, fuck and sometimes the bitch would cook me something to eat. That was what we were cool with just like all my other hoes. So I don't know what the fuck she giving me attitude for.

"Newbie shut the fuck up with that shit for real. You in a whole fucking relationship with a nigga so don't question shit this way," turning my nose up at this fucking girl I was about to leave. She was fucking up my high.

"Alaric stop playing games. You know damn well me and Zae are fucking done. Why do you think you get so much of my time? Come on boo, make me yo' girl," she started putting her whiney voice on thinking that shit was going to work.

"Is you out your fucking mind?! Newbie, the shit we got going on ain't going no further than this. Fuck outta here with that talk," I got up and put my shoes on and she started with that begging shit.

"Ok Alaric I'm sorry. I'm sorry for tripping just don't leave right now. I wanted to spend some time with you boo," I chuckled as I picked up my phone.

"What bitch don't wanna spend time wit tha kid. You fucked that up though. I'll holla when my dick feelin' you again," I grabbed my weed and left out her house. I could hear her getting mad and cussing. Before the night is over, she'll be sending me some nudes and videos saying she sorry.

I know y'all think I ain't shit but let me feel you in. I do like Cassidy a lot. Hell, you heard what my mama said. Lil mama got it all and that shit is fucking rare. But I'm a nigga, a good-looking nigga at that. Fuck good-looking I'm the fucking best next to Jesus Christ himself! No kids are running behind me, I ain't broke and I handle my muthafuckin' business. A nigga like that should have a variety of women at my disposal. My dad taught me that my whole life. Its cool to have one your feeling and might even want to wife up. But it's ok to still have side bitches. You just never give them wife treatment. I don't eat no other bitches pussy but Cassidy's.

I don't kiss on the mouth or cuddle with no bitch but Cassidy. I have deep talks only with her and I text and call only her. I talk to other bitches but its just to let them know I'm coming to get some top or some pussy. I strap my dick up twice when I do fuck these hoes. Plus, me and Cassidy were not exclusive. So shit was cool for me to dip my dick in other ponds. This is what I was always taught and the shit been working for me. Shit the same way Cassidy is a catch, my ass is too. I been caught up before but I'm such a smooth talker. I easily talk a bitch into being back on my team. Simple.

I got into my new Yukon and connected my Bluetooth to my phone. Going to my Spotify app I put on Peezy 56 Bars and pulled off. Summer nights in Detroit were different now than when I was little. It used to be kids still outside playing. Hide n seek, tag, niggas shootin' dice. Shit was still fun in 2004 on the west side of Detroit. Shit, I was only twenty-one, but I feel like my childhood was the last of the fun shit. Hitting the freeway, it was only a little after nine o' clock and I was taking my lame ass home. I really wanted to be up under Cassidy right now.

My dick wasn't working for Newbie because I had my fucking fill today with Cass sexy ass. Shit, I was drained. On my mind right now was Cassidy bad ass riding my dick and squirting all over me. Her sweet tasty pussy was still on my mouth which made me lick my lips. I would call her up and be with her tonight. That thought had to go the fuck away because pimps don't do shit like that. Overnight shit at my young ass age was soft shit and I couldn't have that. My dad would disown my ass. I was feeling Cassidy but one chick life just not something that I was taught. Coming up off the Chrysler service drive I took my exit towards Lafayette to Orleans street.

I lived in a high-rise apartment complex in downtown Detroit called Lafayette Towers. I loved my spot because I just opened the blinds to watch the Detroit Fireworks. The Thanksgiving parade and I was by Belle Isle park, The Detroit Riverwalk, and some clubs. Loved living downtown in my city. Parking in the parking lot I noticed Yatta's truck wasn't parked. That fool probably at his baby mama's hoe ass house. That was another true city rat and I hate my nigga slipped and gave that bitch a kid.

As I walked in the lobby my phone went off. I looked at it as I approached the elevator and saw it was Cassidy. She was asking me if I was busy and that she missed me. As soon as I was about to respond my phone started ringing. It was my dad telling me he had some bitches and wanted me to meet him at Greektown casino. Shit, it was obvious who was going to get a response. Stepping in the elevator, I hit the top floor of the 22-story building headed to my apartment. I was about to get fresh ta death, spend some money and climb into some new pussy.

Zamir

"Z can I ask you a question please?" I was fixing my basketball shorts after getting some dome from this bitch Tia. Tia was Yatta's baby mama best friend. Birds of a feather most definitely flock together. Tia was just as much a city rat bitch than Cleo and her friend Newbie, one of Alaric's hoes, was. When Yatta got Cleo knocked up I made a note to be careful with Tia's ass. Don't need no bitch walking around with my nut in them. I stopped fucking her all together and just got some fire head from her.

"You can speak when you wanna speak. Just tread lightly with your words and we good," without looking at her I put my foot in my Jordan's RE2PECT gym shoes. I don't know what this bitch had to ask me but she had about two more minutes of my time.

"Why is it that we haven't gone pass the physical. All you do is get what you need from me and you bounce. I'm not worth more?" I take the shit I said earlier back. She didn't have two minutes of my time left, she had two seconds. Not even bothering to answer I pulled my phone out to text as I walked to Tia bedroom door.

"Really Z! You'll be that fucking rude and ignore me?" I put my phone down and took a deep breath in and out. This hoe was really pissing me off.

"Tia I'm going to say this shit one fucking time. Every fucking bitch I talk to is only good for pussy and some dome. Nothing more nothing less. No dates, no phone conversations, no cake bake shit. Hell, a bitch can't even sit in my fucking truck or get something off the dollar menu from me. It's always been that way and it will stay that fucking way," I made sure to look this bitch in her eyes without blinking so she could know I was dead ass. Just looking at me she shook her head and chuckled. I turned around and picked my phone back up off her tall dresser. There was no more words needed. I sent my text off and was about to open the door until this hoe had to keep fucking testing me.

"Oh, so I'm good enough to suck yo' dick but Dreka gets your time? That fat bitch-----,"

SLAP!

I slapped the fuck out of that bitch so hard she fell backwards on her bed. Fucking bitch just had to keep fucking pressing the issue. I walked over to her and grabbed her by her blue weave. Pulling her to my face I spoke through gritted teeth.

"Don't you ever fucking disrespect her like that again. As a matter of fact, her fucking name shouldn't even leave yo' dick suckers. Ya' feel me?" she didn't even answer me. She just looked at me with anger. Tears were running down her face and she was holding the side of her cheek. I grabbed her closer so we were nose to nose. I was looking at this bitch like the scum she was.

"DO YOU FEEL ME?!"

"Yes," she said the shit low and she rolled her eyes but I didn't give a fuck. As long as she said yes then we were cool. I let her go and picked back up my phone and keys.

"Have that mouth wet when I call," I said to her as I walked out her room.

My bad for letting y'all see me lose my cool with that rat bitch. But a nigga like me who has had the upbringing I have is just angry at the world. First off I'm Zamir or if you wanna keep ya life its Z. Only two people call me Zamir and we'll get into that shit later. I'm a Detroit nigga born and raised. I love my city and will beat the breaks off a nigga for talking down about my city. Shit, its bad every fucking where in every fucking state. Niggas mad, the job market is low and all the attention is focused on downtown and the suburbs. Bitches having kids and the daddy either ain't shit, in jail or dead. Leaving the mother to raise her kids with no male role model which fucks us up. And I'm speaking on some not all for those who reading this and turning their noses up.

Anyways, those kids grow up and either join gangs, have dead-end jobs, become criminals, or pop out babies and hop in the welfare system. My mama is one of those bitches who has done it all. Cassy filled y'all in on that bitch and ya witnessed first hand how ruthless she can be. But I refuse to let me or my baby sister fall under any of that bullshit. Well, a nigga is a first-class thief, but you get my fucking point. Cassy was my heart and has been ever since I was two-years-old and she was one-year-old. We were only a year apart but the world would think we were years apart. I had always been a big nigga because my pops is a big muthafucka. At 6'5 300lbs I was solid as fuck with tattoos all on my arms and a few on my hand.

I was always the biggest in every grade I was in. For that reason, my pops taught me how to fight. I don't mean no throw a punch or two. You see my pops used to train heavyweight boxers Evander Holyfield and Roy Jones Jr. Google them niggas if you don't know who they are. When I was five he put me in the ring and the rest is history. My ass ain't fight professionally but I had some skills that would fuck you up. I know you're even more mad at my big ass for slapping that bitch, Tia. Well, guess what, I don't give no fucks. I will be the first to admit that I will slap the shit out of a thot, a city rat, and a bitch. I won't close fist a bitch but I'll give a trick my palm in a minute.

Blame my mama for my upbringing. Even though my pops was around. I only saw him on weekends when I was a kid. Being an adult, I see him whenever I want. We were close but not in a father-son way. That was my homie and that's all there is to it. I could have left and stayed with him when I was little. But no way in hell was I leaving Cassy with that drunk bitch. Cassy still had love and a heart for our mama. Me, I just hated that bitch and wanted nothing to do with her. She treated me and Cassy like shit because our fathers were father and son. Nobody made her nasty ass do no shit like that. I was a spitting image of my pops and for that reason, she was more fucked up towards me.

But I can take the shit as long as she doesn't fuck with my sister. I wanted to beat her ass when she hit Cassy but I know my sister wouldn't want that shit. I guess because of the way she treated us I just hated women. Don't confuse my words with a nigga being gay. Hell, fuck no! I just felt they all were thots either looking for a come up or can't keep their legs closed. Look how my mama did. The bitch fucked a father and son! And then got knocked up! Rat behavior at its finest. Then she treated me and Cassidy like shit, kept different niggas around and drunk her problems away. Shit was deep between me and her but I don't feel like talking about that shit now. Just know if it wasn't for my sister, our mama would be dead.

Everybody knew how I was about Cassidy Zarena Collins. I didn't play about my sister and even in elementary if you made her cry. I was fucking you up with my shovel and pail. That shit my drunk ass mama was saying about me being dumb and retarded was far from the truth. A nigga was smart as fuck. Straight A's in school and honor roll every card marking. I don't know how but school came easy to me. Yatta and Alaric used to come to me for help in school. Speaking of them fools. We met in kindergarten and because I was the biggest. They always felt like they were untouchable. Those my day ones though. I could have gone to any school but I wasn't leaving my sister. So, I enrolled in Wayne State University for business management. I wanted my own boxing training gym.

I was making that shit happen to. All I had in life was God, me, my sister, my day ones and Dreka. Let me tell y'all about Dreka Hudges fine ass. I been wanting that girl since freshman year in high school. That damn Dreka is so fine with her juicy sexy ass. Niggas my age act like they didn't want a bitch with some stretch marks and a little stomach. Some extra arm fat never scared me off. As long as you weren't sloppy and kept ya maintenance up then I'd holla at a BBW chick. Dreka was sexy with her shit standing at about

5'6 she had this pretty ass mocha skin. The shit didn't have not one mark or bump on it. Her teeth were pretty and white which made you feel good when she smiles.

I think what turned me on was how girly she was. She stayed looking cute as fuck. Nails, feet, and hair always looked good. Even when she wore her long hair which was my favorite. She looked cute as hell and her voice was so sweet and soft. Shit drove me crazy! Her shape was like an hourglass with just a few extra minutes on it. She had wide hips, a little meat on her stomach and the sexiest round face you would ever see. When she smiled or laughed her high cheekbones would rise. Shit was the cutest thing ever. That was my baby girl all fucking day. I just didn't want to take it beyond a friendship.

Dreka was the only girl next to my sister I let call me Zamir. I hated being around her because of how she made me feel. But the minute I'm not around her I want to be. Shit was wild. I trusted Dreka and she made me see that all chicks ain't fucked up. But I just think if I take it out the friend zone she would switch up on me. I know my size and my exterior made you think I was dead inside. But I'm actually sensitive as fuck and don't play about my feelings. I never had a girlfriend, never been on a date and never pursued a bitch. Nope, I ain't got time for that shit. The games, roles, tricks, cheating and bullshit that comes with all of that.

Naw! Y'all can have that shit. I would fuck a bitch up if she hurt my feelings or cheat on me. I'd kill the nigga and put her in the hospital. So its just best I stayed single. Dreka wasn't my girl so I never stopped her from talking to other niggas. I just slowed the process down. Like in high school, niggas knew not to step to her. She never knew this but I threatened all of Central high school. I put word out that no nigga was to ask Dreka to prom. Her ass end up going with Cassidy and Erin on some group shit. Call me crazy but wait until that nigga Yatta holla at y'all again. He a few screws loose to he just not as harsh as I am.

Anyways, I would get word that Dreka was talking to

some nigga. She would go on dates and entertain niggas. I would always fuck the shit up. One nigga took her to a concert at the Fox Theater. As soon as he dropped her off I followed him home and stole his car. His ass still didn't go away so I broke in his house and took a lot of his shit and trashed that bitch. I dumped it all at the city dump and left him a little note telling him to fuck with another bitch. He got the hint then and stepped the fuck off. My list goes on and on but that's just a little taste of what I have done to niggas who thought they had something coming from Dreka.

I don't know why I was doing it knowing damn well I wanted us to stay friends. I just found myself filled with jealousy whenever I heard about her and a dude. I knew I couldn't carry on with the shit forever. Eventually, she is gone get a nigga and the shit will stick. Then Ima be sitting here looking stupid as fuck. Scratch that shit, I'd just make his ass disappear and she would have to be single forever just like my ass.

Tia lived on Manor and Puritan on the Westside. I had a few minutes to drive to Dreka's house on seven-mile and Livernois area. It was after eleven at night and for some reason before I went home in Canton, about twenty minutes from the city. I just wanted to see her and talk to her. Since tenth grade year in high school I would pop up at Dreka's house late at night and we would just talk. Shit started when she spent the night with Cassidy when we were living with my mama. That bitch came home drunk and threw up all over the living room floor. Cassidy was sleep so I put mama to bed and cleaned up. Dreka came downstairs and helped me. We talked and the shit was cool.

I had never opened up to anyone before about anything. Even with Cassy or my day ones I would just say I'm straight and keep it moving. With Dreka, it was just different. She was genuine, and her beauty made me an open book. I didn't get into deep details about my mama but I would tell her the basics. But any and everything else was on the table. Whenever I'd have a fucked-up day. A good day or

I just needed to rant I'd hit her up and I'd come over. Sometimes she would be sleep but she would wake up for me. Her pops, of course, didn't know we were doing this. Her grams did though because she caught me sneaking out before. She was cool as fuck about it though.

Sometimes Dreka would hit me up and say she needed to talk. No matter where I was or who I was with I was there. If I was out of town on business than we would facetime or just traditional talk on the phone until she fell asleep. As many times as we have talked all night watched a movie together and been close. We had never done nothing physical. A hug was the most we had ever been intimate and I wanted to keep it that way. I think she did too because she never brought it up or tried anything.

Pulling up to her house I texted her and told her I was outside. She immediately texted back and said to come on in. Dreka's dad slept on the third floor of the house and she had the whole basement. The side door was personally hers so that's how I came in and left. Walking up to her house I checked my surroundings and opened the door. Closing the door I made sure it was locked and I walked the stairs down to her room. Dreka had two sides to her basement. One side was sat up like a mini salon. She had a Beyoncé room divider that went around her whole bedroom. I opened it and she was sitting up on the bed watching TV. She gave me that high cheek smile when I walked in.

"Your tall ass is almost touching my ceiling," she joked as she got up and gave me a hug. I wrapped both of my arms around her waist. She had that same smell that I loved on her. That Victoria Secret Love Spell shit. One day I asked her and she told me. Women loved that damn store. Whenever I took Cassy shopping she would have my ass in them for hours. I hated that damn store.

"Shut'cho short ass up. How's your night baby girl? You know I'm about to kill some of that Chinese food you got?" I told her as I kicked my Jordan's off.

"I already knew your big ass would be hungry. I got

plenty so come on," I watched her sexy ass get her little foldable table. Dreka had on some short ass pajama shorts and sports bra. Her ass in them shorts was right as fuck. And that sports bra was supporting her D-cup titties like Trump supported the Klan. Shit was fucking my mind all up. That's what was sexy about Dreka. She embraced having a little extra weight. If you ask me she was thick with a stomach but whatever it was she embraced that shit. She wasn't scared of her body.

"Its late as fuck and I know you didn't go out on Oakman and grab this food yourself. So, who grabbed this for you?" I know I shouldn't ask questions to shit I didn't want the answers to, but I just had to know. She side-eyed me and sat down on her bed next to me.

"You so nosey but if you must know some little dude I met at the shop. He brought his daughter to get her hair done and he tried to holla. Nothing serious but he cool," she said the shit like it was no big deal. It was a very fucking big deal to me. Now my ass was hot as fuck ready to fight. *Calm down nigga*, I said to myself.

"That's what's up. Nigga bringing you greasy fried rats, he couldn't care that much about you," fuck all of y'all who reading this and laughing. Call me a bitch in my feelings I will gladly wear the title. I was in my feelings, jealous and all that other gay shit. She chuckled and said.

"Says the nigga that's eating it with me! And for your information, I asked for Chinese food and he was nice enough to bring it to me," she playfully rolled her eyes at me but I was still salty.

"Why you didn't just ask me. I'd have at least brought you something to drink," *Issa bitch my nigga. That's what you sounding like right now. Get it together.* I pushed my thoughts away and waited for her to answer me.

"Zamir, I asked for this food *before* you told me you were coming. And just so you know he brought me my favorite Faygo Orange pop. When she picked up two cans of orange pop I started to throw them bitches against the wall.

"You a'ight over there, you look a little green," she chuckled and bumped my shoulder with hers. I smacked my lips at her.

"Baby girl ain't nobody green over yo' ass. I'm just talking shit to you. Anyways, how was your day?" I wanted to change the subject. Dreka was having me in my feelings and that shit wasn't cool. I didn't need her thinking she had me that way and then play on that shit.

"My day was good. After me and Erin left Cassidy's house we went to Hayden's house and then I dropped her off," my eyebrow arched when she said Hayden's name.

"I thought that nigga was in Alabama playing football?" I put some more of her sweet and sour chicken in my mouth.

"He was but he hit Erin up and said he was home for the summer. We stopped by to see him for a minute. They been out of high school a year before us and he still is crushing on Erin. It's cute," she laughed while opening her orange pop. I took the liberty of opening her other one. I knew she would be annoyed.

"Did I tell you to open my other pop nigga?! Besides, I haven't had any in three months so I was saving that one," she playfully rolled her eyes and turned her nose up. That shit made me laugh.

"Shut yo' ass up lil nigga I do what the fuck I want. And why you haven't had your favorite pop in a while?" I asked as I almost downed the little ass can.

"I'm kicking that shit so my face can stay clear. Plus, I been working out so I won't get sloppy. Ya know I gotta keep the niggas in my direction," smiling and sticking her tongue out she snapped her fingers. I lowkey was annoyed at her nigga comment but I hid that shit.

"Baby girl in every way shape and form you are perfect. Don't get too skinny on me Dreka or Ima beat yo' ass," we both laughed and those pretty cheeks rose up when I complimented her.

"Let me find out you been lookin' at tha kid,"

nudging me again with her elbow she laughed and blushed. Shit, I was fucking feeling Dreka. I was feeling her tuff as fuck but I couldn't act on that shit so I played it off.

"Yo' conceited ass. Aye, but as you can see, I'm in need of some TLC on my head. Can you hook yo' best friend up?" I threw that best friend comment in there to see what she would say.

"Come on *best friend* you know I got you. Zamir you know if me and dude get serious we gone have to chill on our late-night meetings," I was putting my wallet and phone on her nightstand when I shot my head up at her ass quick as fuck.

"We ain't chillin' on shit Dreka so erase that shit from yo' dome," I didn't mean to get mad and raise my voice but she had me fucked up.

"Now you know damn well your little fits don't ever fucking faze me so chill on yelling," I watched her little chunky ass get up and grab her hair stuff. Them shorts were short as fuck and her big ass thighs were jiggling like Christmas bells. Shit was hot ass fuck with her big booty looking like a snack. Dreka wasn't lying though, she always called my bluff when I called myself mad at her. She never did like the rest and either ran another way or try to kiss my ass and get back on my good side. Not Dreka though, she would laugh at my ass or boss up like she just did. Shit turned me on.

"Come sit'cho long ass down," Taking my shirt off I sat down on the floor between her legs. Between me and y'all I always took my shirt off so I could feel her warm as skin against mine. That's why I never came to her shop and got my hair re-twisted. I had shoulder length dreads that I only let Dreka do. Not even my sister could touch my dreads.

"Who does Cassidy think twist your hair? I know it's not me because she would have blasted my ass," she asked as she separated my dreads. I was about to take enjoyment out of my response.

"She thinks Tia does it," what the fuck I say that for.

"Ah, shit! What the fuck girl!" I looked up at her with an angry ass face. She was looking pissed too but shit I'm the one who just had my hair pulled hard as fuck.

"That bitch ain't got the skills I have. I swear Zamir if you let that bitch touch your hair I'm not fucking wit'cho ass no more," I started laughing.

"One, that shit will never happen. Two, make sure you don't spill none of that green you got going on in my head," she smacked her lips and popped me in the head. I just continued to laugh. Dreka hated Tia even though they have never had an encounter. Her ass was jealous as hell and I enjoyed that shit.

"Whatever. So what, any nigga I get just gotta except my big ass best friend as well?" I nodded my head and she laughed. Dreka started my hair and we chopped it up. This is what I loved. The good convo and vibe we had. Shit was a whole vibe that I knew I would never have with any other bitch. I told her about earlier with my stupid ass mama and Cassidy. Dreka got as mad as I did.

"No disrespect but I'm so sick of y'all fucking mama. Like that shit don't make no sense. I will link up with Erin tomorrow and we will take Cassidy out for the day. Go shopping and eat so we can get ready for Yatta's party," I told her that was a good idea and that I gave Cassidy some hundreds to do it up.

"You're such a good big brother Z. Like for real for real you the shit," I tilted my head to the side and looked at her.

"What I tell yo' ass about calling me Z? Cut that shit out Dreka?" She smiled at me which made me almost smile. I shook my head and went back to letting her do her thing.

"My bad *Zamir* its habit because everybody else around us calls you that."

"Well, you ain't everybody so cut that shit out," I purposely sat back so her pussy could be on my back. Her warm ass thighs and soft skin felt good as fuck against mine. This shit was hard as fuck not to fuck her every time we chilled. Dreka and I kicked it even after she was done with my hair. We watched a movie and she fell asleep around two o' clock. I watched her until around three then I bounced. I don't know why I even did this shit knowing I had a job to do with my day ones at five o' clock in the morning. Oh, well, I'm a 'G' so I can run off of no sleep. I needed to see baby girl.

***

"Damn Unc, Havoc wasn't lying. Ain't shit out here but woods and road. This would be a good ass place to dump a body," the three of us looked at Yatta like he was crazy when he said that shit. We were all in the van driving to Grand Haven. We were in an all-white van with no windows and a DTE logo on it. Havoc made sure we had DTE badges, tools and everything that made us look legit. He was at his house in Novi getting our buyers ready for all of the shit we were taking.

"Alaric what's the address again?" Lonell asked while he drove.

"16550 Rich street. Should be coming up on your right," as he said that we pulled up to the only house in the area. It was big as hell and from the Zillow app, it was a six-bedroom home worth six-hundred-thousand dollars.

We parked the car and like Havoc told us the Japanese family who lived here were not home. They were on vacation in Chicago. We still couldn't take our time because that was just too risky. Getting out of the van Alaric stayed out front to disable the alarm for us. Once we were close enough to the home he was able to tap into their security software. He had eyes on the inside of the house and the surrounding area. He also cleared the area for having and camera up by the light poles and traffic lights. Myself, Lonell and Yatta got up to the door. Yatta did his magic with the locks and within seconds we were in.

"Shit. This house is one of the good ones. Smells like new shit all up and through it. A'ight y'all, let's get it," Lonell said and we started with the living room.

"We are gonna want to take both of those vases. One's a blue Baccarat that's eleven-grand. The other is a hand-crafted porcelain, that's about thirteen-grand," I did what I was good at besides lifting heavy shit. Told y'all I was smart as fuck. Give me a subject to study and I will have that shit down pack in a month tops. This was what we did and I knew in order to make sure we weren't ever cheated. I studied a lot of vintage and expensive shit. Shit that had value and history to it.

"We need to snag these Chinese Swarovski crystal figurines. That's about five-hundred per figure especially if we get an old ass lady to buy them. Roll those rugs up to," I said as we entered the sitting room.

"This authentic Persian rug is hand stitched, that's about ten-grand. This 10x16 one is at least twelve-grand." Yatta and Lonell be fascinated as fuck knowing how much shit is worth. No matter how many hits we did they still couldn't believe I knew all of this.

"These rich muthafuckas insurance carriers are going to be pissed," Yatta laughed as we started taking shit out to the van. We were quick as hell and clean with our shit.

"We still good Alaric?" Lonell asked and Alaric gave the thumbs up. He was watching the area and the cameras down the road leading to the house. We always wanted to make sure no cars were coming. Going back into the house we got to the dining room and the kitchen.

"Grab them Dynasty dolls out that case. Them lil bitches are china glass and worth thirty-five-hundred a piece. Yatta those five bottles of red wine, snag that shit. That Domaine Leroy is eleven-grand. The Domaine Georges and Christophe Roumier is around fourteen-grand," we loaded all that shit on the truck. While Lonell was making sure the items were secured me and Yatta went back in the house.

"That's an emerald princess-cut ring which is nine-grand. Snatch that pearl gold necklace off that mannequin. That shit gone run about seven-grand. Oh, and all four of these short ass statues. These are carved wood, Quan Yin,"

Yatta looked up at me with his face scrunched up.

"What the fuck is a Quan Yin?"

"It's some shit Buddhist put up. They believe it brings relief for those who are suffering," I told him as we headed out the house. Yatta laughed.

"Albert Einstein ass nigga," he joked.

"Fuck you, if you get ya head in a book and out some pussy you may learn some shit," I joked back as we loaded the van up.

"Ain't a book on earth can teach you how to be this nigga here. I'm that fuckin' truth!" His cocky ass pointed to himself and laughed. Once shit was all good in the van we all boarded up. Alaric turned the alarm back on. He cleaned his software of all connections to this area. Pulled back the cell phone towers back up. And we were out. I was ready to go home and fuck the shit out of my bed.

Dreka

BUZZ!

The guards buzzed me and my daddy into the visiting room. We both walked in the room and scanned it looking for my mama. Angelica Reta Green aka my mama was serving a life sentence. In 1998 when I was two-years-old my mama killed a woman that my daddy called himself moving on with. Shits crazy as fuck right? Well, my daddy wasn't always an engineer at Chrysler, he was once a street nigga. Selling drugs, gangs, guns, the whole shebang. My mama was a dancer and made serious money. She traveled with her shit and did a lot of celebrity parties. Anyways, my parents never really had a relationship. They were both young, hot in the ass and they hooked up. Mama got pregnant and my daddy told her she wasn't about to terminate her pregnancy.

They came up with an understanding that they would just co-parent. I guess my mama didn't hold up to her end because word got back to her that my daddy had a new girlfriend. My mama spied on daddy and saw the girl. She followed the chick home and stabbed her two-times. My mama didn't even run and hide. She called the police and waited for them to pull-up and arrest her. Sometimes, I have resentment towards her because every girl needs her mama. But my amazing daddy made sure we both visit her three times a month. No bullshit no matter what me and him have going on. We make the time to visit my mama and she loves it. Sometimes Erin, my uncle E and grandma would all take the drive to Ypsilanti with us.

It feels like I have never missed a beat with her because of how close we are. My daddy and her still flirt and shit together. That's another thing I love about my daddy. He never once blamed my mama. He told me that she was in love with him and he was in love with her but they were both just young. He told me women love hard and mama just couldn't control her emotions. Daddy stayed looking out for her. He put hella money on her books. Had her a good ass lawyer fighting to get her out of here. My mama crime was just evil and premeditated as her lawyer would say.

Regardless of the fact she still was my mama. I love her no more or no less and I don't even have any anger towards her anymore. As far as I'm concerned, she was just staking her claim. Even though a life was lost Angelica Reta Green was still my mommy. I shook my head at the female guards, the prisoners and even the damn visitors gawking at my daddy. The shit had been this way my whole life. People say he looks like Morris Chestnut all the damn time. He was tall as fuck just like my uncle E, Erin's dad. He had the low waves, chocolate complexion, straight white teeth and the goatee. I still don't see it and personally, I find it gross that anyone would want my daddy in that way. Yuck!

He may have looked like Morris Chestnut but he had the personality of Terry Crews. Minus that gay shit, my daddy was funny as hell. His personality and humor will keep you laughing all day. In a nut shell, Delon Hudges, my daddy, was my best friend next to Erin and Cassidy. We were mad close and I love being the only child. I had my daddy all to myself and I loved it.

"Oh, my goodness Dreka you get prettier and prettier," me and my daddy both turned around smiling when my mama walked over to us. She was still so pretty with her long curly hair in a low ponytail. Our complexion was the same blemish free mocha. Her shape would put all the video bitches bodies to shame. Flat stomach, wide hips, huge ass booty and a gorgeous face. My mama was stunning even in light dickie pants and a white t-shirt. You just couldn't hide her shape which thank God she passed it down to me. I just had some extra meat in certain places.

"Hey, mama! And I get it from you so give yourself the praise," we both smiled as we hugged each other tight. She smelled my hair like always and I smelled the Dove on her like always.

"Jelly don't act like you made this girl yourself," my daddy joked. Mama pulled away and put both her hands on my face. She was smiling big as she softly held my face in her hands. Leaning forward she gave me Eskimo kisses like she has done since I was little. Looking up at my daddy she smirked and smacked her lips.

"Shut yo' ass up Delon. I know who the fuck was with me in that black old school that night," when she said that I almost threw up. They hugged and like always my daddy squeezed her booty and I hurried and took my eyes off that nasty shit. I looked at the women looking like this was a free peep show. We were all sitting down and like always mama sat next to me and locked her finger in with mine.

"Jelly you know I'm getting you out of her soon, right? Charles is getting close with his strings with helping me. You need to be home with Dreka," I smiled at my daddy and looked at my mama. She was smiling as well.

"I know Del. Emmanuel came up here with my lawyer last week. I'm ready to be home with my cheeks," looking at me she squeezed my hand and kissed my high cheeks.

"And I swear I am different Del. I'm not going to trip on how you live your life. Hell, the second thing I'm doing when I do get out it gettin' some d---," she stopped her sentence when I act like I was about to throw up.

"My bad cheeks, mama been due for some testosterone," we both laughed and my daddy got mad.

"Shut the fuck up Angelica. Stop talking like that in front of Dreka, and you ain't about to be out here doing shit. Don't let me being legit fool you-----," he looked at me and stopped his words. I know my daddy, he was pissed.

"We need a private visit next week. I'll be up here Tuesday," I looked at my daddy and at my mama faces.

"Oh, my God y'all, this is just sick. Daddy, give me the card so I can get us some food. That way you can talk nasty to my *mama* without me having to hear," I shook my head and stood up as he gave me the reloadable card. Walking up to the vending machines I looked back. Only to see my daddy next to my mama whispering some shit in her ear. They have a sick ass relationship and I want no part of it.

***

After a great visit with my mama, I was on my way to Greenfield Plaza in Oak Park. The Plaza had a lot of salons and other vendors who rented space from them. There were clothes boutiques in there, people who only sold hair. Nail salon renters, jewelry stores, and hair salons. Other shit was in the three-story building too. I worked at a shop called Glamz. It was cool and I made a lot of money. I was just ready for my own salon. Stepping out on my own wasn't even a fear I had. I was a beast at what I did.

I could do any and every hairstyle you throw at me. I was sick as fuck with some scissors, clippers, hair dye, perm. Whatever you needed I promise you I could slay. My only reason for not having my own salon is money. I made enough for me to live and support myself. But I wanted my own building as a salon. Not some rented space inside a building someone else owned. I could have gone to my daddy. I just felt like he already has my mama legal shit on his hands and that was enough.

One day though, I was going to have my own salon. I had a name and everything for her and I couldn't wait. Parking my Sonata, I made sure my doors were locked and I had nothing of value left out. These grimy niggas had no problem breaking into ya' car or just take the whole car. I didn't have time for none of that.

"Drekaaa! Hey gorgeous!" Soul was another stylist that worked at the shop. He was straight believe it or not. The nigga was fine and because of his looks and skills. He kept clients even after hours. Although he took all forms of payments if you know what I mean. Soul didn't play that gay shit and if you came at him wrong, that was ya' ass. Nigga stood at six-foot even but was build and looked just like Curtis 50 cent Jackson. He was fine as hell and may have had a tiny thing for me. But nawww! I can't be mixing business with pleasure.

"Booskie boo! Hey! I didn't know you were opening today. Where is Domonique?" Domonique was our annoying ass owner. She was cool as hell but handled business a little messy. The only reason she stayed poppin' was because of me, Soul and her other three stylists and one bomb ass make-up artist. Domonique could do hair good as hell to. But she always had her clients waiting long, she canceled a lot and chased her dog ass nigga all over Detroit.

"I don't ask shit that ain't got nothing to do with me. She asked me to open and my second job scheduled me off today so here I am. I leave all that bullshit gossip to y'all," I laughed and gave him a hug. He wasn't lying though, Soul didn't gossip or start shit. The only time he talked to us is if we are talking about movies, sports or music. And even then, the minute we start talking about a nigga being fine. His ass would put his beats on or connect his Bluetooth to the smart TV and listen to the sports channels while he did hair.

"Dreka when you gone stop playing and go out with me? Yo' juicy ass is so sexy and you know we would make fine babies," Soul always said the same shit to me when we were alone like right now. He just has never been this close in my space like now. I was standing in front of my station. He crept up behind me with his warm breath in my ear. Thank God it didn't stink because if it did I would have had to read him his violations. Instead, I just smirked and side-eyed him.

"Soul you have more than enough girls to keep you busy. Stop focusing on little ol'me and focus on opening up the store. You know I don't mix business with pleasure," I said to him. He wasn't touching me but he was all up on my ass and the side of my face. I could feel him smiling as he smacked his lips.

"Man Dreka for yo' curvy ass I will drop all these hoes and only take cash or card," When he said that we both laughed. The door opened and Tia walked in with August.

Oh, I forgot to tell y'all! Tia was an assistant at the same shop I worked at. Me and her couldn't stand each other. I hated her because she was a gutter ball bitch. Working here was her side hustle because she also danced at Ace of Spades. August was ok, she never said no sideway shit to me but she fucked with Tia heavy and for that, I was good on her. I don't get down like that. If Erin or Cassidy don't like a bitch then I don't like the bitch either. Friendship code!

"Soul yo' hoe ass always trying to push up on Dreka and she stay curving you. What up Dreka girl," August joked as she playfully bumped Soul. He waved her off and winked at me. I shook my head smiling and spoke to August. Not even giving Tia the time of day I got my station ready for my eleven-a.m. client.

"Damn I thought Domonique had a dress code for us. When clients walk in here it should be to some professionalism," Tia smart ass made her comment out loud as Soul turned on the radio and TV. I did a inside laugh and continued setting up.

"Tia cut the shit," Soul said as he swept up some hair off the floor.

"Why the hell are you sweeping booskie, you know that the helps job," I was talking to Soul and pointing to Tia since she was just an.

"You fat bitch what'chu tryna be funny?!" When she said that I cracked the fuck up at her basic ass.

"Bitchhhh please come harder than that. You been itching to call me fat because that's all you will ever have on me. And you know that's not really having shit because you work for this fat bitch. Matter of fact, go clean the fucking bathroom. Fucking help!" When I said that this dumb bitch tried to come at me. I stood right there waiting on her to get close enough. I was going to mop the floor with her ass.

"You think you all that you big hoe! I bet this one thing, you gone stay the fuck away from Z! He is all fucking mine!" I threw my head back laughing when she said that shit as Soul held her back.

"Bitch I ain't even in the way. The nigga just want nothing more from you but top! He don't even want yo' stretch arm strong pussy!" Tia tried to reach over Soul and get to me. I was sick of this shit so I punched her ass in the fucking nose. Somehow she got over Soul and tried to pull my hair but tripped and fell into August station. Jumping up she charged at me and we were fighting. I don't know why people always tried to come for my hair. It's like they mad because my shit is just as the same as the bundles I wear.

"YOU STUPID BITCH! STAY THE FUCK AWAY FROM Z!" Soul broke us up as August pushed Tia into our supply room. I had on some ripped shorts, combat booties, and a plaid button-up. My hair was in a curly side ponytail.

"Gorgeous calm down boo. Fuck that bottom bitch and her lame ass mouth. She just be fucking with you because shit just look at you. Tia is fucking jealous. Go fix your hair and let's continue our day. I'm sending her home," Soul said as he let me go. I was so fucking mad but I did like Soul said and fixed my hair. I could hear Tia in the supply room yelling shit. I fixed my hair, grab my phone and stepped out the salon for a minute.

"Baby girl----," I cut Zamir off before he could even finish. I was so fucking mad and this shit was getting old.

"I just got into a fight with your bitch. I'm so tired of this hoe smart ass mouth all because she thinks me and you are more than friends," heated and talking fast I paced the floor as I ranted to him.

"Slow down Dreka, what the fuck are you talking about? I ain't got no bitch," his heavy voice was making my eardrums shake.

"TIA! You know exactly who the fuck I'm talking about. Look, I think our friendship is cool and all but maybe we should just end it here. Tia gone end up in the hospital if she come at me again and I'm talking to somebody anyways. This shit is getting ridiculous Z," I calmed down a little the more I walked.

"Hello?" I said into the phone because Zamir was so

quiet.

"Dreka I don't know who the fuck you raising your voice at but when dealing with me. You better always come correct. And you betta stop fucking calling me Z. Now, I'm sorry you got into a fight with Tia's dumb ass. I'll handle it and I promise she will not fuck with you anymore. Ima assume you bleeding from your pussy as a reason for you telling me that me and you gotta stop chillin' like we do. Don't say that shit to me no more baby girl. I'll handle Tia and I will see you tonight at Yatta's party," with that, his ass hung up on me. I looked at the phone like I didn't know what it was. I saw Tia barge out the salon and march to the elevators. I don't give a fuck what Zamir says something was telling me that me and Tia were just getting started with this shit.

Erin

      The weather was perfect as noon came around so I decided to drive to the Detroit Riverwalk and get some drawing done. I wasn't in a painting mood so I took my pack of number two pencils, my beats headphones, and my phone. I haven't drawn in three days and that was too damn long for me. The Riverwalk was one of my favorite places to draw. All I needed was the perfect scene and my mind took a picture of it. I didn't even need to take my eyes off my paper once I saw the perfect scene. If I was at home I would have locked my bedroom door and painted topless the last memory of New York. Instead, I wanted to be out in the sun and the fresh air.

      I took out my seventeen-inch drawing sketch pad and pencils. Taking my headphones out I put them in my ears and went to my Spotify app. I was in an Anita Baker mood so I played her greatest hits and looked at the scene in front of me. My mind blocked out the few people who were on the Riverwalk walking. I never drew people for a few reasons. I prefer to draw nature and animals. A beautiful sky or this beautiful river that was surrounding the Riverwalk. Canada was across the river and I noticed a flock of seagulls in the sky along with a plane that trailed two thick white lines in the clear blue sky. The sun was placed perfect and the trees that were around me looked healthy.

      I pressed my back against the steel chair I was sitting in as the Detroit Princess boat blew its horn. I saw some other boaters in the water as well. Their boats were giving the water some pretty waves. I had my scene in my head. Pressing play on my phone Anita played in my ears as I opened my sketch pad. Since I couldn't be topless I had on some basic black leggings with a PINK sports bra and some mint green and white Puma gym shoes on. As soon as my pencil touched the pad I felt at peace. I love drawing and painting. At times my love made me an outcast in school or on social scenes. I was called weird or a white girl trapped in the hood all because I loved to draw and paint. Go fucking figure.

It was in my DNA to have this passion considering both my parents were gifted to. My dad still paints but only does it in private. Some of his pieces were in Henry Ford museum. Not his own work just some paid work for decorations. The only person my dad would paint around was me. I loved when we would break out our pencils and brushes together. It was perfection at its finest. Speaking of my parents, my mother texted me and said she wanted to see me when she got off work today. I really wasn't in the mood to deal with her nasty attitude or her sarcastic ass comments. I figured the sooner I see her the sooner I can get it over with. My daddy was going to be at work so I didn't have him to face her with me. Dreka was at work and so was my uncle Delon.

My grandma couldn't stand my mama and wouldn't hesitate to pull her pistol out on her. No, ma'am! I wasn't in the mood for any of that so my daddy's house will have to do. I was so into my drawing that I didn't even see someone approach me until a shadow covered my sketch pad. Looking up, I almost shitted myself. Yatta sexy ass was in front of me breathing hard and smiling. He had on his blue Beat headphones, some blue Nike shorts, blue and white Lebron gym shoes and no shirt. His chest was wet and that caramel skin was glistening. I wanted to lick the fucking sweat off his abs. Mm! I pulled my headphones down and smiled back at him.

"You didn't hear me calling you? That's not good Erin yo' cute ass need to always know what's going on around you," he sat down next to me and I closed my book. I didn't just let anybody see my freestyle work. Sometimes, not even Dreka or Cassidy.

"I know my dad says the same thing. So, how you

been Yatta? Its been a while," I had to take my eyes off his hard chest. Looking in his fine ass face I don't think that was any better. Yatta was sexy ass hell with his neck length dreads. His straight white teeth were complimented by his sexy ass full lips. His top lip had that dip in the middle and I swear I wanted to suck on it.

"Erin," he said my name and at that moment I realized I was gawking at him.

Fuck, Erin!

"Oh, um yea I will make sure to pay attention to my surroundings," he laughed and so did I even though I didn't know what was funny.

"You didn't hear shit I said, did you? I said I been good now that I'm out of that small ass cell. How was the big apple?" I felt so embarrassed but I tried to play it off.

"New York was good and never boring. The clubs were live the only thing negative about New York is it's expensive," he shook his head at what I was saying. When I looked at him he was doing the same thing I was earlier. Gawking.

"That's what's up ma. I see you're still drawing, keep that shit up girl. I missed seeing you around with that drawing pad," he smiled at me making me smile. That's one thing that stood out to me about Yatta. He loved to smile but he was still so rude. People took his smile and thought he was for the shits but he wasn't. I remember a few times he had to pop off on niggas and bitches.

"So, you're a family man now I heard. Congratulations," I know I was reaching but whatever. I wanted Yatta to know I knew he got that thottie Cleo knocked up.

"Hold the fuck up with yo' slick ass mouth. I have a son, not no fucking family. You know Cleo was never my bitch. Fucking and sucking was all I had her for and the sucking was all was done from her," he scooted closer to me. Eyeing my body while biting his lip he looked up at me and said.

"You coming to my party tonight Erin?" Damn his voice was so low and deep. And even though he was sweaty I could smell his Degree deodorant and his I AM KING Sean John cologne. I never could look Yatta in his eyes and especially with him being this close to me. *Move the fuck over. Actually, move closer and wrap those muscular arms around me.* For me to be a virgin my insides were yarning for him like I knew what to do with him.

"Um, I didn't know about it but knowing Dreka and Cassidy then yes. I'll be there," I scratch my shoulder and fidgeted with my sketch pad. I looked everywhere but at him. All of a sudden he used his index finger and turned my head to him. He had the sexiest smirk on his face.

"You still can't look at me huh? I ain't shit Erin but a nigga. You to pretty to be so shy and nervous. I'm glad your back for good though, I can honestly say I missed you," with his arm over the chair, I was sitting on I looked at his sexy ass face. He had these low dark brown eyes that matched his honey color skin perfectly.

"Why are you glad I'm back?" That's all I could ask in a low tone. He was sitting so close to me. All the years I have known Yatta he has never been this close to me. I was fucking stuck and under a trance. I need to snap out of this shit.

"Ain't nothing standing in my way now. I never wanted to be in the way of you doing your thing after high school. A nigga like me not shit beyond Detroit. Now, I just feel like maybe there is some hope," shit, he had me more stuck then what I was before. I wasn't expecting him to say that. I have always had a thing for Yatta but he was always in some kind of trouble. I won't lie though. It kind of made me think he was just a typical hood nigga who would never be anything. Then he started doing tattoos and piercings. I saw how he hustled that and I was shocked to see how smart he was to get into UCLA. I never even thought college was on his mind.

"Yatta you just had a baby with Cleo. Everyone in

Detroit knows how she feels about you. The drama is something I don't need. Do you have pictures of your son in your phone?" I asked anything to change the subject. He pulled his phone out his pocket and showed me pictures. I had never seen his baby before. Cleo didn't post him on her page. All she had was her turning up, twerking and throwing back shots. Thottie at its best. Yatta's face beamed as he showed me his little boy. He told me his name was K.J. and I must say he was adorable with his chubby cheeks.

"Look, Ima let you finish your drawing. I gotta get out of here and get ready for tonight," he got up and I just admired his sexy ass back. Yatta had a basketball player built and boy did he ever keep the maintenance up on it.

"Girl get yo'ass up and give me a hug," I laughed at his rude ass demand but y'all know I got my ass up. I was only 5'5 and Yatta was 6'1 so he had a little height over me. I thought we were going to do a church hug. He shocked me when he pulled me in wrapping his arms around my waist. My arms just naturally went around his neck. I melted like ice cream on a hot ass day. His skin felt good and he had a grip on his hug. I felt safe and secured like this with him.

"I'll see you tonight Erin," with that he put his headphones on and started back running. I felt like a damn school girl. All smiling and having butterflies. I was really inspired now more than ever . Checking my watch I had another two hours before I had to be back at my dads house to meet my mama. Opening up my pad I continued to draw with this same stupid smile.

***

As soon as my mamas Mercedes pulled up I took a deep breath in and out.

"She never stays long Erin," I reassured myself. I watched from the porch as she pulled into the driveway. I put my phone in the back of my jeans and walked off the porch.

"Is that how you dress now?" As soon as she stepped out her car that was the first thing she said. Not hello, no smile, a head nod or nothing. I didn't have on shit special just a ripped t-shirt dress and some BEBE chunky flip flops. My feet and nails were done and my curly hair was in a low ponytail.

"Hello to you to ma," inhaling out I noticed she had someone sitting in her passenger side.

"Who is that?" I asked pointing to her car.

"That's your brother. He insisted on coming here with me even though I don't know why," as she said that my so-called brother got out the car. My first time seeing this stranger in my whole life and we were in the same state.

"I wanted to come because it was time to meet my sister. Erin, I'm your brother Jamie," he gave me a hug but I didn't even know how to respond to his hug.

"Its time for us to have a relationship if that's ok with you," I gave him a half smile and looked at my mama. She was rolling her eyes.

"That's ok with me Jamie I have no problem with that," he smiled and this time I gave him a big hug.

"So now that you're done wasting your time and money in New York now what? You're about to get food stamps and some dead-end job?" I squinted my eyes at my mama stupid ass comment.

"Actually daddy got me a job----"

"Oh, Erin stop with this 'daddy' shit. You're too damn old to be calling him daddy. Sounds like some freak stuff is going on," before I could say something Jamie chimed in.

"Ma chill the hell out. Erin, I'm sure if you left New York it was for good reason. Let's exchange numbers. I would like to go out to eat so we can talk and get to know one another. I'm sorry it took so long," I smiled at him and pulled my phone out. After we exchanged numbers we hugged and he went and got back in the car.

"Why would you say something like that and in front of him? And for your information daddy got me a job painting and Cassidy got me a job at her store. I don't need no food stamps," I was so mad at my rude ass mama.

Looking at me she started laughing.

"That's so pathetic. Hopefully one day you'll wake up and get out of this city. Get a decent job and maybe a decent guy. You have nothing coming to you walking around with a brush and your head in the clouds. You won't be pretty for long." I looked her in her eyes and shook my head.

"What is your problem with me? I have never done anything to you or anything to disappoint you," I had been wanting to ask her that for so long. I never really knew why she disliked me so much. Yea I know what my daddy tells me but I was hoping she had a different version. Instead, she walked back over to her car. Before she opened the door she turned and looked at me and said.

"My problem is you were born," just as easily as her words left her mouth she easily slid in her car and backed out the driveway. I watched her pull off until she got to the corner and turned into traffic. My eyes filled with water as I replayed what she said and her facial expression. I can't believe she could look at me and say that. To hear the person who birthed you say something so heartless and cold knocked the wind out of me. Wiping my face I made a promise that when I have children. I will make sure to drown them with love that it overwhelms them.

***

"I swear I hate both of the vessels that carried y'all. I'm so sorry both of my babies had to deal with that shit," Dreka said to me and Cassidy. We were in her car pulling up to Fairlane Mall in Dearborn. I had spilled the beans about my visit with my mama. Cassidy told us what happened yesterday with her and her mama. It was so crazy how both of our mamas were fucked up. It was crazy and just sad.

"Well, hopefully, some retail therapy makes you two smile. Just be thankful that the both of you will never be like them two bitter ass women," me and Cassidy both agreed with Dreka's comment. Dreka parked by JCPenny and as we were getting out I decided to tell them about my encounter with Yatta today on the Riverwalk.

"Girl that nigga has been wanting you since freshman year in high school," Cassidy said while she put her Gucci purse on her arm.

"Erin, would you let Yatta take your virginity?" I looked at Dreka like she was crazy when she said that.

"Hell naw I wouldn't. He has a baby mama and a whole baby," we walked into JCPenny and the two of them started laughing.

"Bitch I hope you be more convincing with him then you are with us," Cassidy smart ass said and Dreka was cracking up with her. I smacked my lips and turned my nose up at them fools.

"Forget both of y'all. Just because Alaric and Z can get between the both of them legs as easy as we got in the mall. Don't mean I'm crackin' it open for Yatta," that shut them the fuck up as we got to Forever 21 which was Cassidy's store.

"I hate when I'm off and still see this damn place. Two of my co-workers asked me to do there nails earlier. I'm like I don't want to see no damn co-workers on my day off," she joked. Cassidy loved her job as store manager. Her side hustle was doing nails which she was just as good at. I loved how myself, Dreka and Cassidy had passions and things we were great at.

"Thank you again, Cassidy, for the job. I promise to not let you down," she smiled and waved me off playfully.

"Boo you know I had you and I needed an assistant manager after I had to fire Erika. Her ass was late all the time and I gave her too many chances," me and Dreka laughed at Cassidy because she was walking around the store like she was on the clock.

"Bitch lets get you out of here before yo' ass clock in," Dreka said as we pulled her out the store. We went of course in Victoria Secret PINK store. What girl goes to the mall and not stop in there. I loved Fairlane when it was quite like it is. I hate when teens and my age group are all packed in the mall. It's annoying, someone is going to fight and be rowdy. Anyway, after we left PINK we went to *Dollhouse* boutique, *Cest La Vie* clothing store, and *Manic* shoes. We had some good ass outfits for Yatta's party tonight. Speaking of that.

"So, when were you two going to tell me we were going to Yatta's party? Y'all had me believing we were going to have a lady's night tonight," side eyeing them they both were looking guilty and up to no good. I just smiled and shook my head at them.

"Ok Erin look. It's nothing wrong with being a virgin but boo you clearly like Yatta and he likes you too. We just think you need a little push in the process. Y'all know each other and know what the other is all about. You don't even have to go through that awkward introduction stage. Nothing is standing in the way------,"

"Except for me," the three of us turned around when someone interrupted Dreka talking. Cleo was standing there with her two sisters. She had a scowl look on her face and so did her sisters.

"I'm confused on how Detroit is filled with niggas and you gotta come for one who has a fucking family," she looked at me and said with an attitude and a whole lot of unnecessary anger. Before I could say my what the fuck I wanted Dreka spoke up loud.

"Bitch Bye! You trapped that nigga and got a baby out of his ass. You ain't shit but a vessel and you know it. How the fuck you gone talk about family but don't never have yo' own kid. Look at all them bags. I see not one bag from a kid store. Get'cho raggedy ass on and watch my cousin play step mama to junior," after Dreka read Cleo her rights me and Cassidy broke out laughing making Cleo and her sisters madder.

"You need to shut the fuck up. Thanks to yo' fat ass Z put his hands on my fucking best friend. What the fuck is with you and this bitch trying to fuck with niggas that already have girls?!" she spat. And now it was my fucking turn.

"Exactly what you just said. They have girls and what

they need is grown ass women. Cleo get the fuck out of my face and focus on being a single mother. I got Yatta and soon enough we'll be giving junior some siblings," I could feel Dreka and Cassidy mouths drop when I said that. Cleo looked like she wanted to step to me.

"Do we have a problem, ladies?" Two security guards approached us in the middle of the mall. We were on the first level of the three-level mall. Nobody spoke ass me and Cleo had a stare down.

"Ok let's break this up and have a peaceful shopping experience or we are going to have to escort all parties off the premises," the guard said. Dreka and Cassidy pulled me in the opposite direction.

"Damn bitch I can't believe you stepped to that bitch like that! I fucking loved it!" Cassidy and Dreka high fived me as we walked to the food court. I was so heated with that stupid bitch. See this is the shit I didn't want to deal with. Naw I gotta stay clear of Yatta ass.

"No, let's rewind to what she said about Z and Tia! What the fuck was that about? What's really going on with you and my brother?" Cassidy asked and I wanted to know too. I knew Dreka liked him but not enough to come to blows over him.

"Ain't shit going on. Y'all know Tia works at the same shop as me. Well, that bitch tried to talk shit this morning and we got into a fight. She must have flapped her gums to Z or some shit. I doubt Z put his hands on her and especially over me," Cassidy nodded her head but I knew Dreka better than I knew myself. This bitch was lying on so many levels. Once we get home in private she was spilling all the tea to me.

Yatta

"So let me get this shit straight! My baby daddy comes home missing from jail after missing the first ten months of OUR SON life and I'm not invited to his homecoming party! You got me all the way fucked up!" All I was trying to do was take a shit in peace. This bitch outside the bathroom door yelling at the top of her lungs.

And just to be clear she is absolutely right she ain't invited to my fucking party. That gap tooth bitch I hooked up with that works at Footlocker in Fairlane. She hit my line telling me my baby mama was showing her ass at Fairlane. I told her I didn't give a fuck and I hung up on her ass. She then sent me a flick of the shit and I see Cleo looking at Erin like she was about to fuck her up. I dialed the jump-off back and she tells me security broke the shit up. I was annoyed as fuck at Cleo stupid ass. I already know I was the reason she tried to step to Erin.

Cleo already knew how I felt about Erin since high school. She assumed because I never made a move and I fucked her that I wasn't interested in Erin. But like I said before, I was on some I didn't deserve a good girl like Erin type of shit. Now things were different and I realized I need and want a girl like Erin. The fuck one bitch, cake and bake all on the phone lovely dovey shit. I ain't saying its gone be easy but at twenty-one-years-old, I'm willing to try. I'm not about to let Cleo fuck this up for me. I will put that bitch in the hospital and have her ass eating out of a straw.

A bitch like Cleo was destined to stay stuck in the hood. Have a bunch of kids running behind her and chasing behind some nigga. She thought because her body was banging that she would always win. Bitches like that hate women like Erin, Dreka, and Cassidy. They know nothing but greatness comes from women like that. So for that reason, they hate on them. Shit sad but its reality. Whatever her reason was for fucking with Erin she should have thought twice about that shit. After I wiped my ass good, I sprayed some Febreeze she had in her bathroom and washed my hands. Cleo was still talking shit behind the door. I was going to walk right past her until she said some stupid shit.

"You just wanna be all up in that plain bitch Erin's face! I swear if I find out you were with her you will never see K.J. again!"

BAM!

I knocked her ass in the fucking face with the bathroom door. Her head went back and she screamed while grabbing her nose. Somebody should have gave this bitch an Oscar for best performance.

"OH MY GOD YATTA! CALL 911!" I slammed her against the wall and grabbed her now bloody nose making her scream in pain.

"Shut the fuck up and listen to me. If you ever play with me about my son I will make sure I break more than your fucking legs. You know me well enough to know I would never have randoms around K.J. Erin, however, is not a fucking random. *When* shit go my way between me and her," I put my face closer to hers so she could really look in my eyes.

"Yo' ass is not about to get in the way. You completed your life goal and got a baby outta me but that's where it fucking ends for you. A baby mama and sometimes a warm mouth is all you will ever fucking be to me," I gritted my teeth at her ass.

"Keep yo ass away from my party or I fucking swear," I let her go and walked back in the bathroom to wash my hands.

In case you haven't put the shit together I have a fucking temper on me along with my hate for losing. The shit wasn't a good combo but that's what makes me that nigga Yatta. You would never tell because I loved to smile. Shit, I got some sexy ass lips and some nice white teeth. Why not show that shit off? But as friendly as I looked it still was a nigga and bitch best decision to not get on my bad side. That's why I kept so many bitches because I was constantly dropping them hoes on their heads.

I don't deal with drama, cheating (on their end) and I don't deal with jealousy. When I say jealousy, I mean from me. I have never been and will never be jealous of a bitch and anything she does. I can't even count how many times a bitch would use another nigga to try and make me jealous. The shot never fucking works. I don't get jealous and I don't play games. I just drop a bitch exactly where I left her and move on. And she better hope nobody in her close circle meets my standards because I would gladly move on with them. Drying my hands I walked passed a crying Cleo and went in my son room. He was wide awake smiling and playing in his crib. The TV was on that *Wiggles* show he liked. I smiled and picked his fat ass up just to kiss on him.

"Daddy love you so much K.J. and I'm sorry you have to hear me fuck ya, mama, up. I never want you hot temper like me. I'll see you tomorrow baby boy," he laughed and spit droll all over my face. That shit made me smile and laugh at his cute ass. Putting him back in his crib I looked in his closet and made sure he was straight on everything. I wanted him to live with me but Cleo swear she wanted him with her. I try not to be that ruthless and just take him plus I missed the first seven months of his life. But if Cleo kept this shit up then I was taking his ass and she would have visitation.

"Yatta, why do you keep doing this. Don't you want K.J. to have a family?" she sat on the couch with some Hennessey and a shot glass. I snatched that shit off her table.

"My fucking son is in the room. You not about to pass out.....You know what here you go! Knock ya'self out," I put the liquor and shot glass back on the table. Walking back in my son room I got him a bag ready and got him dressed.

"Yatta where the fuck are you taking my son?!" she

jumped up off the couch looking pissed.

"I'm taking him to your mama house. You gone head and drink and smoke yo life away. You in yo feeling for what? Because we will never be together. Cleo, you not who the fuck I want. Even if Erin wasn't in the picture I still wouldn't want you. Lock the fucking door," I walked out her shit with my son in my arms. Getting to my truck I strapped my baby boy in and got in the driver's side. Cleo's mama was cool as fuck. We got along good and she even knew how her daughter was. I fucked with Cleo's mama and her stepped dad tuff and they were good people who knew their three daughters were some thots and no good. After I drop my baby boy off I needed to get dressed for tonight.

***

Stepping out of my truck I felt good as fuck. Club Bleu in downtown Detroit was packed and all the love a nigga was showed felt even better. You'd think I was a celebrity or some shit the way the bitches were calling my name. My boys and my uncle set all this shit up. All I had to do was get dressed and show up. I was killing it tonight with my Pierre Balmain faded jeans and fitted matching shirt with the logo big as hell on it. Both my ears, neck and wrist was iced out in diamonds. My chain that I wore a lot said 'Yatta' and was damn near blinding. My dreads were freshly twisted by this bitch I fucked with.

I had some Lebron 15 Ghost on my feet looking crispy. I hope y'all put the shit together that I was a Lebron fan. His shoes were the shit and I always rocked a pair. Walking in the blue-lit club I saw the white satin curtains all over the ceiling and the walls. There was a big ass banner saying, 'Welcome Home Yatta' and my picture under it. My niggas and uncle really did the shit up. I saw the buffet of all the food and drinks. The D.J. interrupted the music and announced me as I walked in.

"Attention Detroit! Show some love and bitches show ya pussies for that nigga Yatta! Welcome home my nigga!" Everyone turned towards the entrance and the spotlight was on me. I nodded my head and threw the fist sign to the D.J. as Alaric, Z, my uncle, and auntie walked towards me. They showed love as well and told me the left high level was all our VIP section. I saw so many bad bitches in this muthafucka.

"Yatta, let me give you some welcome home head real quick. I promise to suck the holy ghost outta you," this fine ass redbone said in my ear. I told her to keep that shit on ice for me and I would get at her a little later. You'd a thought I told her ass she hit the mega million with how happy she was with my response.

Getting up to our area I sat down and grabbed a champagne flute and sipped on the Dom Perigon P2. I felt like that made nigga that I knew I was.

"I want to make a toast to my nephew. This nigga is not even my nephew, this my fucking son right here. As long as I breathe I will make sure you never see the inside of a cell again," my uncle stood up and made a toast.

My auntie was right next to him smiling and nodding her head. We toast to me and I gave my uncle a hug. This nigga was right when he said I was his son. He was more of a father to me and I loved his ass for that shit. I gave my auntie a hug and kissed her cheek. She was like my mama and since day one she has treated me as such. My niggas showed love to me as well. After we were done with all the gay shit we turned up

I got one, two, three, four, five, six, seven, eight M's in my
bank account, yeah (oh God)
In my bank account, yeah (oh God)
In my bank account, yeah (oh God)
In my bank account, yeah (oh God)
In my bank account, yeah (oh God)
In my bank account, yeah (oh God)
I got one, two, three, four, five, six, seven, eight shooters
ready to gun you down, yeah (fast)
Ready to gun you down, yeah (oh God)

Ready to gun you down, yeah (oh God)
Ready to gun you down, yeah (oh God)
Ready to gun you down, yeah (oh God)
Ready to gun you down, yeah (oh God)

21 Savage Bank Account was booming through the club and I had a bad bitch dancing all on me. She was working that shit too and shaking her fat ass booty like I was paying her. I looked over and Alaric was in the corner with a bitch who I knew was sucking his dick. Z mean ass was smoking and about three bitches were trying to get his attention. I never understood these hoes wanting to fuck with his mean ass. The nigga gave no fucks, quick to slap a hoe, punch a nigga and shoot you after. But the bitches still wanted to be in his face. Shit was wild as hell.

Bottles popped, weed passed and laughs exchanged I was having a good ass time. I pulled my phone out and it was eleven o' clock. I'm not gone front I was looking for Erin. She told me she was coming and a part of me was annoyed because she was late. I looked over and saw Z on his phone. He stood up and looked down into the crowd. I followed his eyes and saw Cassidy in the crowd. She was moving through with Dreka behind her but I didn't see Erin. Call me a bitch but I was a little mad. Where the fuck was she? I know damn well she didn't blow my party for some other shit.

Cassidy and Dreka came up in our area and I swear Alaric ass almost shitted bricks. The chick he had wasn't sucking his dick anymore but she was sitting on his lap. Cassidy peeped it laughed and shook her head. She hugged her brother and Z big ass was fucking struck by Dreka. No disrespect towards my nigga but Dreka was a bad ass plus size girl. She wasn't even big just juicy as hell. She was wearing the hell out this black fitted dress with long tight heel boots that hugged all the way up her leg to her knees. Cassidy was bad to in this green one-piece and gold heels. Alaric had been pushed the bitch that was on his lap off him. I laughed to myself as the girls walked towards me smiling.

"Hey, Yatta! Welcome home love," Cassidy greeted me and hugged me. Dreka did the same and they both gave me gift bags which I thought was dope as hell. I tried to play the shit cool but fuck that I needed to know.

"Aye where the fuck yo' cousin at?" I asked Dreka over the loud ass music. She leaned over and in my ear and said.

"She here don't worry. Hayden stopped her when we came in so she got at him for a second," let me tell y'all how fucking heated I was.

Hayden whack ass always had a thing for Erin. He was a football player who thought because Erin was a cheerleader that they should have been together. Nigga was lame as fuck and had no game because as many study sessions and dates he has taking Erin on. His gay ass still never locked her down. Now, this nigga wanna come to my party and push up on my bitch?! Naw, not going down. Yea I said my bitch and I mean that shit. Erin was fucking mine and that was that. Before I knew it I was walking out my VIP section looking for them.

Looking around I saw them standing on the floor and he was saying some shit in her ear. She was nodding her head while doing some shit on her phone. I looked in our section and saw Dreka in her phone so I knew they were texting each other. Before I went over there and claimed my girl I took in how good she looked. Erin had these tight ass jeans on that was painted on her. Her pretty ass hair was down all big and curly.

She had these black heels on with a black top. When she turned a little I saw her entire back was out and Hayden had his hand on her lower back. This nigga about to be watching football in Alabama from the stands . Because I swear I was about to break both his legs.

"You want'cho fuckin' fingers broke my nigga?" I walked up on them surprising both of them. I could feel Erin looking shocked but I had eyes on Hayden's bitch ass.

"Tha fuck Yatta, Erin ain't spoken for so why the

fuck you mad?" I grabbed the hem of her jeans and yanked her cute ass to me.

"Yea she is my nigga and if you wanna keep playin' for that chitlin'circuit school you'll keep yo hands off mine," Hayden lame ass held his hands up and looked at Erin and walked away. I looked down at Erin and she still was looking shocked and then she looked mad.

"Yatta, I am not your girl. Hayden and I have always been friends and nothing more. You were so rude!" she yelled in my ear but I see she hasn't snatched away from my embrace. Yea, she was feeling a nigga. Just like earlier when she was gawking at my chest on the Riverwalk.

"How the fuck you gone come to my party, stop and mingle with a nigga before saying something to me?" I said to her and she looked a little sympathetic. Erin's face was so fucking beautiful. She had this smooth skin and nice pink lips. Her eyes were a chestnut brown and I swear I could look at her all day. Straight cutie pie!

"I'm sorry Yatta, I didn't even mean to get caught up with Hayden. He just stopped me and said he wanted to holla at me. You look handsome as hell tonight though and I'm glad your home," when she said that in her sweet voice I softened up. Grabbing her hand we walked back to my VIP area. Dreka and Cassidy were dancing to *Migos Bad and Boujee*. Erin was about to head in their direction but I held her hand tighter.

"You about to chill with me yo' ass has mingled enough," I sat down with her next to me. Looking up all eyes were on me and Erin. She was blushing and not looking at me. I laughed and waved their nosey asses off. Her girls, my niggas, my uncle, and aunt had these goofy ass smiles on their faces. Shit was mad annoying and I wish they would pay attention to some other shit.

"I still can't believe you did----," I cut her off in her tracks.

"We ain't talkin' about that country ass lame. He was in my fucking way and I didn't like it. Anyways, I wanna take you out tomorrow," she was fidgeting looking nervous as she looked at the crowd. I grabbed her chin and made her look at me.

"What I tell you about that shit, I'm just a nigga Erin," she smiled at me and finally looked me in my eyes. I could tell she still was nervous because her fingers were knotted up. Shit was cute to know I had that effect on her.

"Yatta---,"

"Kenyatta cutie pie. Call me Kenyatta," I told her and I swear she turned red as fuck. I never and I mean never let anybody call me by my first name. Teachers, my uncle, my auntie, I don't give a fuck who you were. I would check yo ass in a minute about that shit. Erin was different and she had my young ass gone. All the gay feelings that you read about and see in movies I was feeling. Shit was mad annoying but for her cute ass its whatever.

"Kenyatta, why do you want to take me out? I don't want drama with your baby mama. Clearly, some shit ain't clear on her end. She thinks y'all are a family and I'm not about to get in the way of that," I couldn't help but laugh as I picked up a flute. I passed her one and I sipped on one.

"I want to take you to *Andiamo's* for dinner. We can eat on the water and then catch a movie. Sound good to you?" I looked at her and waited for a response. She took a sip of Dom and shook her head. There goes that nervousness and looking away.

"Cutie pie I need them pretty ass eyes on me," I told her and she was back to looking at me. I saw Cassidy and Dreka on the dance floor. The crowd was having a ball and showing love. I was appreciated but right now, Erin mattered. I had been wanting this shit for a while and now I'm ready to collect.

"Did you hear anything I said. Cleo-----,"

"Stop talking about other muthafuckas that are not important. We talking about you and I's date tomorrow night. You look hot as fuck in this outfit by the way. But all this sexy ass back you got showing and ass poking out is attracting all these niggas eyes. Shit fuckin' up my steelo cutie pie," I lightly pinched her cheek and she blushed again. That shit was cute as fuck which is why I gave her that nickname.

"Ok, Kenyatta. We can go out but I'm going to need you to make sure Cleo is in her place. Or I swear Kenyatta I will beat the mustache off her upper lip," aye, that shit made me laugh my ass off. Not because I thought Erin wasn't about her words. But because she straight threw a damn tree at Cleo's ass. Clearly, Erin thought I was calling her bluff. She smacked her lips at me and pushed my arm.

"Yo, that shit was funny as hell Erin. But check it, I can assure you that Cleo will know she ain't shit but my son mother," I sat up and gripped her chin in my fingers.

"I swear Erin, nigga or bitch will get fucked up if they fuck wit'chu a'ight," I was dead serious and had a serious expression on my face.

Blushing like always she nodded her head yes and took a sip of champagne. We turned up and celebrated my release the rest of the night. Erin thick ass danced on a nigga and I ain't gone lie. I hogged her ass all damn night even from her girls. She was lovin' that shit though. Cleo's sisters were there. They peeped how I had Erin by me and I'm sure like the trolls they are they'll report back to Cleo. Ask me if I give a fuck though. I'm muthafuckin Yatta and I always do what the fuck I want. Just wait until I make Erin mine officially. I was a touchy-feely ass nigga and what was mine was mine. Bitches really gone be mad then, but I dare one of them to say some shit.

***

"Havoc you sure these niggas legit?" I asked him as we waited in this open field on Greenfield and Curtis on the west side. Havoc met up with my uncle a few weeks before our hit in Grand Haven. He told him these three niggas came highly recommended by one of our buyers in D.C. They were professionals like us and agreed to share their listings of homes, auction showings, and jewelers for a price. Today we were meeting with them to see if we all wanted to get down. My uncle never does shit if we all don't agree on it. He always says that's how shit fucks up.

"Yea lil nigga they legit and it's going to be a lot more money in it for us. They are brothers and the two owned the same D.C. buyer we deal with a favor and he put in a good word on our behalf. I just need you and Godzilla here to be on chill," he said pointing to me and Z. We both looked at that fool like he was crazy.

"Aye nigga when you speaking on me I gotta fucking name. And the last time I checked my pops at the crib and even his old ass can't tell me how the fuck to act," Z baritone ass said to Havoc. My uncle just shook his head and laugh as he ate his apple. Havoc and Z didn't really get along because sometimes Havoc tried to act like he our father. That shit didn't sit well with us especially, me and Z. Alaric is real laid back and he will blow you off before he loses his cool. Me and Z were quick to fight or shoot. So fucking what!

"So, you and Erin," Alaric ugly ass smiled as he smoked on his Jazz Black and Mild. I folded my arms and shook my head at him. I knew one of these fools were going to start with this shit.

"You had her booed the fuck up last night. What's poppin' wit that my nigga? Y'all a thing or some shit?" my uncle laughed as he continued to eat his rotten ass apple. Z did a light chuckle and so did Havoc. Alaric smiled big and goofy as he waited for me to answer.

"Fuck y'all nosey asses," I waved them off and pulled my phone out.

"I mean if she a free agent then let Hayden-----,"

"She ain't no fucking free agent my nigga. Erin is fucking mines! And why you speakin' on that lame nigga I will break his legs six different ways if he goes near her. Now nigga relay that shit back to him since you speaking for that lame!" Alaric, my uncle, and Havoc fell out laughing. Z big ass did his annoying light chuckle. That was the closest to a smile or laugh that his mean ass would give you. I turned my nose up at these stupid ass niggas. Shit wasn't funny.

"That's what the fuck I thought bitch! Quit frontin' like you ain't feeling ma," I was about to get on Alaric ugly ass when a white Charger pulled up.

"That's them," Havoc said and we all got together ready to meet these niggas. Two tall dudes got out the car and walked towards us. Havoc spoke first and introduced us all. Instantly, shit didn't feel right. I don't know what the fuck it was but I just didn't feel right around them. I looked at Alaric and Z and they gave me the same look. They weren't feeling it either.

"So as Havoc explained to you we are willing to share our list with y'all if we can get a cut. We are very good at what we do and have a client list of buyers outside of the U.S. All we would want is our cut," the one Havoc introduced as Simon spoke first. I looked at his brother as he spoke and he kept glancing at Havoc and then at my uncle.

"Where y'all from again?" I asked them.

"Me and my brother are originally from Flint but we reside in Tro now," when he said that I gave that nigga the stink face.

"Oh y'all from Flint?! So if I stick y'all two in a dark room will ya' glow in the dark from all that fucked up water?" I smirked and asked. Alaric fell out laughing and my uncle tried to hide his laugh with his arm. I stood there staring at both of them waiting on an answer and Z big ass did his usual light laugh.

"Aye yo' Havoc this lil nigga needs to be taught some respect," the other brother named Silas snarled. That's all it took for me.

"You wanna try to teach me muthafucka," I walked towards him and instantly Z and Alaric followed.

"Come on fellas lets not forget about the purpose here, money. Come on now Yatta please chill out," Havoc bitch ass looked at me and pleaded.

"Fuck this shit, I ain't doing business with them. As far as I concerned I don't even know why we here," I said to

Havoc while looking at these two simple Simon ass brothers.

"Alaric, Z y'all feel the same?" My uncle sat on the hood of his Cadillac truck. They both agreed and that's all my uncle needed to hear.

"Deals off fellas," he threw the rest of his apple in the field and walked around to the drivers side of his truck.

"Come on Lonell man, we ain't even heard shit out yet!" Havoc started whining making me shake my head. I knew my uncle was about to get annoyed. His temper was worse than mine and he had lesser patients.

"You heard my boys nigga don't fucking act brand new! I'll get at yo' ass in a few weeks!" he spit his words like venom as we pulled off in his truck. Leaving the simple Simon twins and Havoc standing there. Something just don't feel right about them mercury drinking niggas.

Cassidy

"You ok boo? You seem somewhere else?" Erin asked me as we both dressed some mannequins in the window display of my store. When I say my store, I mean Forever 21 but since I'm the store manager, it's my fucking store. Erin had been working as the assistant manager for five days now and it was working out great. My girl was a fast learner, good with customers and although nice she made sure the rest of the staff worked. In no time she would be able to open and close on her own.

"I'm good just a little tired and ready to go," I gave her a smile that I knew was weak.

"Girl bye, now what's wrong Cassidy?" I looked around for a minute at the store and saw it was a little slow. It was a Sunday morning and Fairlane is usually slow on Sunday mornings. Then I thought about it, nobody knew about me and Alaric. Hell, Z doesn't even know and I didn't want him to find out from the streets. But now after Yatta's party, it might not be shit to tell.

"Cassidy!" Erin called my name and snapped me out of my thoughts.

"Erin if I tell you something please don't tell anybody. I know you and Dreka are cousins but I really want this to stay on the low."

"I got you boo, I promise," I chuckled and began telling her about me and Alaric. I told her about how I had been feeling him for a minute. How he popped up at my job and asked me out. How we had spent time on the phone and chilled together. I told her we smashed a lot of times and recently last week. Then I told her about Yatta's party and the bitch that was on his lap bothered me. I saw when he tried to push her off but by then I had seen enough. Plus, his pants were unzipped. I know how my brother and his boys got down and I'm far from stupid. Z made sure I knew how niggas moved and thought.

"Oh, WOW! I wasn't expecting you to spill a gallon of tea. I stand by my promise to not say anything. I just want to say this and I hope you don't get offended," I nodded my head and waited for her to speak.

"Alaric is cool as hell and I have never had a problem with him. But he is his father's son. That pimp, women ain't shit mentality. As fine as he is Cassidy I think you can do better and I see nothing but heartbreak and games coming from him. Whatever you decide I'm rockin' with'chu I just want you to be careful," I appreciated Erin for saying that to me. I knew all about Alaric's daddy and his womanizing ways. All of Detroit knew about how he ran through the young and old girls. I heard his sex game would leave yo ass crazy. And he had a lot of money so that made women go even crazier. He always reminded me of Denzel Washington when he played in the movie *Training Day* his looks, walk, and personality matched perfectly to that. A true asshole.

"I understand what you're saying boo and I'm not offended. I been knew about Alaric's dad and his shit. I just thought I was different and caught myself catching feelings. He's been blowing me up but I don't have shit to say to him," I saw Erin's eyes bucked. I turned around and Alaric was walking in my store with a fucking girl. This could not be happening right now. Like is this nigga fucking stupid?!

"Bitch look at me," Erin said and I turned back around in her direction.

"This nigga is looking for a reaction and being messy as hell. Keep yo' shit calm and sexy but know I'm with you and following your lead," she told me as I felt a mean ass fucking mug on my face. I was ready to fuck Alaric and his blonde head bitch up. I got my shit together and put my big girl panties on. I swear my slim thick ass body was so hot but I was looking good as fuck today so that made me feel better.

"Hi, welcome to Forever 21. Did you need any help

today?" I asked them with a big bright smile. Alaric grabbed her hand and looked at her.

"You need help boo?" *BOO!?* I said to myself. Oh, this nigga is reaching?

"Um, I'm looking for a nice outfit for the Xscape concert next weekend," Blondie looked at me and said. She was not the cutest but her body was nice. With a gap and a somewhat big nose, she was light skinned with long blonde tracks and chocolate brown highlights. Erin was behind them pretending to fix clothes on the rack.

"Ok just tell me your style and I can see what I can do," still wearing my million dollar smile she began telling me.

"Wellll, I like something not to old and covered up. Its summer time so keep it sexy and revealing and I like shiny stuff," I couldn't help but laugh at her high pitch hoodrat voice. We began walking the store and I helped her piece together an outfit. Ric was so annoyed and every two seconds he would smack his lips, turn his nose up or shake his head. You see Ric wanted a scene. He wanted me to either run and cry, act a fool on her or act a fool on him. Naw bruh, you gets none of that from me.

"Ooo girl this skirt is all the way fleeky and this top you picked is so me. Do you have any earrings or body chains?" she asked as she admired the outfit.

"Girl you know we do, I actually am about to go in the back and grab some new body chains we just got," I excused myself and walked towards the back.

Erin was helping two girls but she kept eyes on me. I winked at her and she nodded and smiled. We really did have some cute body chains that would go nice with the outfit I picked out. Because I chose blondie's outfit out I must say it came together nice. I grabbed a box cutter and opened one of the boxes. I heard the door opened and I assumed it was Erin or Mora my other girl who was scheduled today. The next thing I know I'm being swung around.

"Why the fuck you playing with me?!" I was shocked

as fuck to see Ric in my back room yelling at me.

"Ric what the fuck are you doing back here and why the fuck are you yelling at me!?" Thank God I didn't have all of my staff here. This shit was so unprofessional and ghetto. I'm also happy my district manager was on vacation. I'm just going to pray to God that a pop-up visit from corporate wouldn't happen right now.

"Fuck all of that shit Cassidy answer my question. Why the fuck are you playing with me? Do you know who the fuck I am? You been dodging my calls and ignoring me. And now-----,"

"Now what nigga?! I ain't giving you your show you want?! You had a bitch suck yo' dick at Yatta's party and then she was sitting on your lap. You damn right I ignored yo' ass and then to make matters worse you show up at my job with a bitch on your arm," he started to laugh and that shit pissed me the fuck off.

"Ric get the fuck out of my store. As far as I'm concerned me and you are done! Whatever the fuck we had is dead," I was fighting hard as hell not to cry. I wasn't even hurt I was more so angry. Angry at myself and at him. Ric looked at me with so much anger and his nostrils flared like a bull.

"Cassidy I—I don't do shit like-----," he kept talking but stopping all while still holding my arm. I looked in his eyes and saw a confused look. Like he was unsure of how to form his words. I also saw fear, pride, and a huge ass ego. As if he saw what I saw he immediately switched his face back to anger.

"You know what, fuck you, Cassidy," he tossed my arm and got ready to walk out before I said.

"Nigga its been fuck you!" Looking back at me pissed he walked out. A tear fell from my eyes because I was so mad and a little hurt. Erin walked in and looked around for me.

"You good boo? I saw him leave and snatch his bitch up by her arm out of the store. What the fuck did he do to you?" I wiped my face and told her what happened.

"Girl as far as I'm concerned fuck Ric and all of his bullshit. I'm glad this happened before I caught real feelings and invested some real time," I told Erin. She smiled at me and nodded her head. Me and her finished our shift and I tried to get Ric bitch ass off my mind. I had took myself off the market for him. It's about time for me to get my pretty ass back out there and do me.

Alaric

"What the fuck you bring me to the mall for if we weren't going to buy anythingggg?" I almost opened the passenger door on this bitch and pushed her out. I hate a whiney bitch. All Neshia did was whine behind every sentence. Shit was mad fucking annoying.

"Neshia shut the fuck up. Don't talk no more until I drop yo' ass off and even then wait until I pull off," she sat back in the seat of my truck pouting and folding her arms. Trippin' ass bitch!

I was pushing the fuck out of my truck on the freeway. I was ready to drop this bitch off at her crib and go hang with my dad. This shit with Cassidy had me so fucking livid. I can't believe she played me like that. At Yatta's party, I didn't even know she was coming. Z never said shit and Yatta never said shit about Erin coming. When I saw Cassidy its not like I kept entertaining the bitch who sucked me off. I pushed that bitch up off me and told her to go downstairs with the rest of the party. Shit, I don't fucking do! I had an ounce of respect for Cassidy and how the fuck does she repay me?!

By ignoring my ass the entire party. She didn't even speak to me or acknowledge my existence. I'm fucking Alaric James Bell! Every bitch acknowledges me and if they don't they must be blind or fucking retarded. Naw scratch that, a blind bitch sixth sense would kick in and a dumb bitch would gain the IQ of a genius. But not Cassidy, she flat out acted like I wasn't there. Dancing on niggas in her tight ass one-piece she had one. I can't front though she was looking bad as hell and it would have been dope as fuck to see us together. The only reason I didn't pop off was because of my nigga Z.

He still doesn't know me and Cassidy have a thing.

But him being her big brother, he was shutting down some of the niggas that were on her so I was happy. Between you and me, through the night at the party, I would snitch on Cassidy to Z if a dirt nigga was all up in her space. I tried to make it seem like I was looking out for baby sis. Truth be told I was looking out for me. I don't know what the fuck was happening but I was feeling a type of way when niggas were on her. After the party, I did go to a room with that bitch that topped me off. Hell, I'm entitled to do me. But Cassidy is NOT entitled to do her. She was a woman and needed to behave as such.

The next day I called her and tried to see if she wanted to go out but she didn't answer. I took it as if she was at work or just busy at the moment. Cool, no big deal. But then the day went on and I called and texted her again. Still no answer or respond to a text. We both have an iPhone, so it said she received and read the messages. I just put two and two together and realized she was ignoring me. I popped up at her crib but I never saw her car. Shit had me so fucking over baked with anger. No bitch has ever and I do mean ever ignored me.

After calling and texting every day I decided to pop up at her job with this Susie from Rugrats looking bitch. I knew Cassidy would be at work and I figured what better way to get her attention. I wanted something from her, a scene, a mean look, something to show she gave a fuck. But what the fuck did she do, straight played me. Smiling and delivering good customer service like I wasn't just deep in that pussy a week ago. Cassidy was doing shit to me that no female ever had done.

I controlled bitches, it was my craft. Even without giving them the dick, I controlled them with just a look. So ya' damn right I followed her in the back room of her store. Only for her to tell me to get out and we done?! DONE! I ain't never been fucking dumped or dismissed! Naw, not me! Not Alaric! Fuck that, fuck feelings and fuck Cassidy. Shit was good as dead and I'm making it my business to forget about her. Turning down Joyroad on the Westside I pulled up to this bitch house. Putting my car in park I pulled my phone out to send a text and hit the unlock button.

"Damn Alaric you not gone come innnn?" she smacked her lips and started that pouting shit.

"Naw, but either you get out or I push yo' ass out. I got shit to do darling," still not looking at her as I texted. I hate a hoe that don't get the hint. I could hear her taking her seat belt off.

"Well, we still going to the Xscape concert right?" I chuckled and put my phone on my lap.

"I don't wanna see them old fat hoes try to sing. Watch ya fucking feet before I run them bitches over," I said as I pulled off. I was done with her ass and likely wouldn't hit her up no more. I shot my dad a text and let him know I was on my way.

***

German Alaric Bell was my dad and also that nigga I wanted to be like when I get old. No homo but the nigga didn't look, dress, walk or even speak like he was fifty-five-years-old. He had a mixture of old and new school swag. Not to mention money and bitches out the ass. To top it all off, he was a good ass father to me. I was his one and only child so he wanted to make sure I was a reflection of him. I didn't mind because he was a real-life GOAT(Greatest Of All Time) next to Yatta's uncle Lonell. But don't tell my dad I said that shit.

Anyways the nigga taught me all the shit I needed to be that nigga. Besides good looks, he taught me how to dress. Never overdress and never wear how much money you have or come from. Look good as fuck and do ya' thang just don't overdo shit. I learned every man should have at least two good three-piece suits. Never know what cause for the occasion. I demanded attention anywhere I went and I was never the loudest in the room. And the Bitches, aw the bitches! I had every bitch I ever came across eating out the palm of my hand. Shit started when I was three-years-old and would never stop. All teachings of German Alaric Bell.

"Son, what's poppin' baby boy!" I walked in my dad big ass living room. He had this nice ass home on Ridgeview in Novi. His shit was nice as fuck but you could tell a woman's touch made the shit feel like a home. You know how y'all women know how to coordinate and make shit come together. I walked over to my dad and embraced him with a five and a hug.

"What's good dad! What the hell Ginger cooking, shit smells good as hell," I asked him as I sat down on his couch. Ginger was his twenty-one-year-old wife. She was bad as fuck with her chocolate ass. Thick as a stack in my pocket and her face was fucking carved by some Gods or some shit. I tilted my hat to my pops for snaggin' that. I mean he cheated all the time and did him but Ginger got wifey treatment.

"Shit I don't know you gotta ask her. Ginger! Ginger get'cho ass in here and say hi to your step-son," I laughed every time he said that shit because me and her were the same age. She walked out the kitchen smiling while on her LG Bluetooth around her neck.

"Let me call you back girl, I'm on mommy duty," she said to whoever she was on the phone with. I laughed and showed her some love.

"What you back there cooking ma dukes?"

"Some ox tails, wild rice, and cabbage. You staying?" she asked as she sat on my dad lap. He was smoking a cigar, sipping on his Crown Royal.

"Yea he staying and then he gotta dip because I'm tryna dip in----," I scrunched my face up and held my hand up.

"Come on pops I don't wanna hear that shit," him and Ginger started laughing. She got up and went back to the kitchen. Even though she was my age and fine as hell I still looked at her like my dad's wife. Now, me and my him have shared bitches before but wifey was off limits.

"Nigga how the fuck you think you got here? So,

what's been new?" He asked me as my phone vibrated. I had it in my hand so I just looked at it and saw it was a random so I ignored it.

"Shit, me and my niggas had to meet up with these lames that Havoc claimed had a cash flow listing. Shit didn't feel right when we met them so we deaded that shit," my dad knew what I did for a living and he respected it. Hell, he was still in the drug game so he never judged.

"That was fucking smart, remember what I told you about going with your first mind," he said as he put his cigar out. My phone went off again and I checked it seeing it was yet another random. I looked at my dad TV and saw he was watching the movie *Training Day.*

"You know the offer is still open to work with me if shit ever gets to slow for y'all. That big nigga Z would make some good ass muscle," I shook my head at my pops as he talked. He always said me and my niggas could make some easy money with him. We never had to because we were living good off of our operation.

"I know dad, good lookin' on that," I said as my phone vibrated again. I looked at it and hit ignore.

"What's the deal, nigga? You keep jumping every time that phone goes off?" I could have smacked myself. My dad always watched everything and never missed shit. I wasn't in the mood for a lecture so I played it off.

"No deal, just don't wanna miss no money," that nigga looked at me like I smelled like the bullshit I was spittin'.

"Fuck outta here little nigga with that lying. Who you think you talkin' too? You came from my nut sack. I know when yo' ass lying and I also know what good pussy will do to a man. I also know what pressed look like. What's her name?" I looked at him and shook my head. He didn't give a fuck about her name. He was about to clown my ass and get mad because he *thinks* I'm pressed.

"Man dad it ain't nobody----,"

"Nigga what's the little bitches name?" I don't know

why when he said that I got mad as fuck. Now my dad was a well-built guy. Not all buff but he was board shoulders, stood at 6'3 and I was 6'2 even. He could lay my ass out but he wouldn't do the shit easily.

"Dad chill out for real. I said it wasn't shit," he stood up and putting his glass down."

"Who the fuck you tellin' to chill out?! You sittin' in my face looking like a true bitch made nigga because a hoe ain't calling you?! I didn't think I had a daughter I thought I had a SON! A FUCKING REFLECTION OF ME! And you wanna sit here, pout and check me for calling the girl a bitch! STAND THE FUCK UP!" I stood to my feet and was face to face with him.

"You letting another nigga stand over you!? This bitch knockin' you off ya square that hard!" I got heated with him calling Cassidy a bitch. My dad started smiling.

"Aww shit nigga, look at the fire in ya eyes. What you in love? You wearin' yo heart on yo' bitch ass sleeves?" He started teasing and laughing. I was so fucking mad I swear if my gun wasn't in my truck I would have shot his ass. He stepped closer to me still smiling.

"That fucking girl that got you in yo' feelings is weakness. And I ain't raise no weak ass nigga. Drop that bitch-----,"

"SHE AIN'T NO FUCKING BITCH!" I pushed him and before I could regain my stance he hit me with a closed fist in my jaw.

"GERMAN!" Ginger screamed and ran to help me up. My dad started yelling and talking shit.

"Acting like a fucking bitch over a bitch! You gone try to step to me nigga! Get'cho ass up!" Ginger gave me a towel so I could wipe my lip. I stood up with so much anger and I was ready to pop. I tried to remember that this was my pops and I didn't want him dead. I stood up while looking in his eyes. I gave Ginger the towel and I headed for the door. I was done with this shit. I could hear my pops laughing and screaming.

"LOOK AT MY BITCH ASS SON! WALKING
AWAY WITH HIS DICK TUCKED BEHIND HIS LEGS!
YOU CALL ME WHEN YOU GET'CHO BALLS BACK
FROM THAT BITCH!" Even out his door I still could hear
his ass laughing and talking shit.

I got in my truck and looked in my rear-view mirror
to check out my face. My lip was still bleeding. Reaching in
my glove compartment I pulled some tissues out and cleaned
my lip. I was fucking livid and ready to blow this nigga's
house up. Swear my dad can sometimes be so fucking extra. I
pulled out of his driveway and into traffic. I needed to smoke
and take my mind off of all bullshit. Fuck German and fuck
Cassidy.

***

"You ready to talk about yo' lip nigga?" Z asked me
while we sat in his living room smoking. Yatta was on his
way from dropping off his son. I was going to my crib but Z
hit my line asking did I want to smoke.

"Shit me and my dad had some words. You know
how that nigga is," I took a pull of the good ass loud and
passed it to Z who was nodding his head. Z and Yatta knew
how cool me and my dad were. But they also knew how he
would be quick to snap if he felt I was being soft for a bitch.
My dad fell in love one time, she cheated on him and he been
on some fuck bitches type of shit ever since. He'd disown my
ass if he even thought I was soft for a female. Even though he
was married to Ginger, he wasn't soft for her or in love with
her. She was just wifey and got the perks.

"So before Yatta get here I gotta rap wit'chu about
some shit," Z said as he passed my back the blunt. His 70-
inch TV was on NFL Network on mute and his Amazon
speaker was playing *Icewear Vezzo* album through his condo.
Nigga lived in Canton which was the suburbs but he still
played his loud ass music. I think because of his size people
left him the fuck alone.

"Speak ya mind," I told him.

"When were you going to tell me you been fucking Cassidy,"

now, I ain't no scary nigga but I had a little jump in my heart when he said that shit. Cassidy must have told his ass.

"Look Z, I wasn't on no disrespect shit. Me and her were trying to see where shit would go first before we told you. Plus, I know you know how I roll with bitches," his nostrils flared and as he took a pull of weed.

"My thing is you know how I feel about my sister. You was getting' yo' dick sucked at Yatta's party when I assume you and Cassidy were fucking. Am I right?" he asked with some sarcasm in his voice.

"Yea we were but she ain't fuckin' with me no more because of that. Whatever we had is over," I stared off for a second before I said. "She dropped my ass," maybe it was the weed because I was being mad honest.

"So you did treat her like these randoms that you fuck? Look, I'm not gone go back and forth about this shit. Cassidy my sister and off the strength of you being my day one. Ima let you live, but Alaric," he looked at me with a snare.

"Either do right by my sister or leave her the fuck alone," I nodded my head as I took the blunt out his hand.

"I already decided to leave her alone Z. You ain't got shit to worry about on that. I figured she was gone tell you," I wasn't even mad at her for telling him.

"She didn't. I noticed how you pushed ol'girl off of you when Cassidy and the girls came to Yatta's party. I ain't no dummy so I put the shit together," I laughed at what he said and shook my head. A knock came to Z door and he got up to let Yatta in.

"Y'all ain't gone believe this shit!" Yatta came in pissed off. I gave him the blunt to calm his ass down. Z and myself rolled up five blunts so we were good.

"What the fuck Cleo do now?" Z asked while he sat back down in his recliner. I was sitting on the couch and Yatta was standing in front of us looking pissed.

"Nigga take a puff and clam down," I joked and told him. He did and shook his head.

"A suit was outside my apartment building," me and Z whole demeanor changed. A suit was a cop. Not a nigga in a traditional blue cop uniform. A desk nigga, a detective or worse.

"He was watching you or he said something to you?" I asked.

"He ain't say shit to me except good morning," me and Z turned our noses up in confusion. Yatta smacked his lips and said.

"Look, I came out the towers and the nigga was parked next to my truck. He was sitting on the hood of his white Charger eating a sub sandwich and drinking a Pepsi. Its hot as fuck out so he didn't have a jacket or nothing on," he was pacing the floor holding the blunt while he talked.

"He was a black fat Uncle Phil lookin' nigga. He had his badge and gun on his hip. I was side eyeing the nigga as I walked to my truck. As soon as I was about to get in my shit he looks at me and goes. 'Have a good evening Mr. Bailey' while still stuffing his fat ass face," when Yatta said that shit me and Z looked at each other.

"Tha fuck type of shit?!" I said and we went quiet for a minute. We were all careful about our shit. We didn't talk about it outside of us, never with a bitch and we didn't showboat. We lived good but nothing noticeable.

"You tell Lonell yet?" Z asked and Yatta said yea.

"He wants to meet with us tonight. Shit was off as fuck. The nigga called me by my last name and shit. How the fuck we get heat on us?" Yatta asked but we knew it was more like a statement. We got quiet for a minute and just took what Yatta said in. Jail was never a fear because it came with what we did. The only thing in question is we never slipped up. We were careful as fuck. Shit wasn't right and I had a feeling that this was only the beginning.

Zamir

"I swear I'm so sick of this bitch! Even after I put my foot up her ass she still blows my phone up!" I was getting so annoyed with Tia's ass. Swear bitches will get hung up on some good dick. I never took this bitch out or nothing. She ain't even had no dick since Yatta knocked her best friend up and she still stuck on me.

"That's what you and Yatta get for fucking with them thottie thots. Sooo what's this about you snapping at Tia about Dreka," I looked up at my sister while we sat at her marble kitchen table I got her for Christmas. I had stopped by to check on her and bring us some Popeye's chicken to eat. Cassidy was sitting here eating and smirking waiting on me to answer. Smart ass.

"Ain't shit, I hate a loud mouth bitch," I shrugged my shoulders while still eating.

"Z come on big brother. I know you feelin' Dreka and she told me what happened at her job with Tia. Why don't you stop playing and take Dreka out?" I almost choked on my food when she said that. Cassidy passed me my drink so I could get my shit together.

"Man Dreka is the homie just like Erin the homie. I'm not checkin' for her or any other chick that way," Cassidy tooted her lips up at me.

"Why you lying Z? And, since when do you drink orange Faygo? That's Dreka favorite," my annoying ass sister looked at me cheesing.

"Shut yo' ass up and eat. Dreka ain't patten orange pop. I just had a craving for the shit."

"Mmmhmm," her slick ass said.

"Anyways don't act like I didn't have to find out about you and Alaric on my own," she gave me that sad puppy face when I said that. Cassidy could deal with anybody being mad or disappointed in her but me.

"I apologized about that Z. Stop bringing that and your loser ass friend up," when she switched up and got mad I chuckled.

"You was feeling him huh?" I asked her that and her eyes got watery. I got mad as fuck but had to remember that I couldn't kill my day one.

"Cassy, I told him if he means no good by you to just step the fuck off. I mean that shit, you ain't about to be like these bitches running behind him," she started fanning her tears back in her eyes.

"I won't Zamir you don't have to worry about that. I actually have a date Friday," I looked at her and she smacked her lips laughing.

"He's a good guy Z. His name is Jamil, he's twenty-four and he works at our college. He's really sweet and he asked me out so I said yes," looking at my sister she seemed happy and that's all that matters. We finished eating and chilling for about an hour before I kissed and hugged her bye.

In my truck on my way to check on the boxing gym, I managed on the Westside. I couldn't wait to have my own boxing gym. Getting some of these kids off the streets after school may decrease some of the foolishness going on in the streets. I know when I was in high school wasn't shit to do after school but get into trouble. I had big plans for my gym and even thought about putting some gymnastics or some shit in it for girls. It's still in works but I know soon I'll bring it to reality.

I thought about us meeting up with Lonell yesterday. That damn suit that was outside of Yatta's apartment threw us off. That shit just wasn't right and out of all of us why Yatta? We had questions that we knew no answers to. Lonell told us not to worry about it he was going to be on it. He had some eyes and ears on the police force so he would find out what was up. Meanwhile, he told us to keep acting smooth, we all had legit jobs so to keep going to them. I asked about our hit in D.C. Lonell told us once he gets word what's up with that suit nigga then he will let us know.

"Z you gone teach me how to box like you?" This little kid named Jeremy was six and he loved boxing. Whenever I'd decide to suit up and box he would be so loud and hype.

"I'll teach you lil homie but you know it takes time and patients. As long as you keep doing good in school then we got a deal," I told him as I helped him put his boxing gloves on. He smiled with his missing ass teeth and said deal.

Most of these kids were dropped off because their parents didn't want to be bothered and wanted the break. I can't tell you how many times I volunteered to take kids home because their parents forgot to pick them up. Only to see the parents at home drinking, smoking, fucking or partying. Shit was sad as fuck but it's what some bitches and niggas do. Faris owned the city boxing gym and only charged a fifteen-dollar a day fee if you wanted to bring your kid to the gym. He always fed the kids, talked to them and made the shit fun. He was dishing out more money than he was making but he loved to do this.

I coached four of the kids and let them get in the ring. Some teens came in and we had our peer meeting. I made that shit up and Faris was cool with it, Basically, I chopped it up with the teens and since it was all guys we talked about it all. Sex, home life, bitches, beef and everything. These teens, in my opinion, are misunderstood and were giving a rough start. No pops in the home, mother works a lot. Some of them have grown responsibilities and not even sixteen-years-old yet. It was cool bonding with them and choppin' it up. Me and Faris ordered Jets pizza and pops(or soda for those who call it that shit) for them to drink. I didn't do this for a paycheck because y'all know how I make my money. I just loved the boxing and being around the kids. Shit was dope.

Back in my truck I texted my sister and checked on her. She told me she called our stupid ass mother and checked on her. That bitch claimed she missed me and Cassidy and wanted to see us. She knew who to say that shit to because I would have hung up on her ass. Cassidy Facetimed me begging me to go. I swear my sister always did this shit but I wasn't letting her go back over there herself. I hated that me and her didn't have the type of mother we saw on TV. Y'all know the aunt Viv from *Fresh Prince Of Bel-Air*. Or Clair Huxtable from *The Cosby Show* those mothers were the truth. Hell, I would even take Florida Evans ugly ass from *Good Times*. All I knew was------WHAT THE FUCK!

I turned down Dreka's block only to see her outside with some nigga arms around her waist. I made sure my pistol was on my waist. I couldn't park my truck quick enough. I swear all I wanted to do was chill with her and go fuck my bed. Now I gotta fuck this lame ass nigga who I assume is the nigga that brought her the Chinese food up. I didn't call or let her know that I was coming but I didn't give a fuck. I was breaking this shit all up and still chillin' with her tonight.

"Aye!" I made both of them jump with my heavy ass voice. I looked at this yellow ass nigga and his ass turned pale as fuck. Bitch born nigga.

"What the fuck is this?" I asked pointing between the both of them and looking dead at Dreka.

"Um, Zamir why you didn't text me? And this is Carter, Carter this is-----"

"Her nigga," I interrupted her sentence.

"WHAT!" They both said loud and in unison. I looked at that nigga staring his bitch ass down.

"Zamir don't fucking do that. Carter, this is not my boyfriend," Dreka's eyes were bucked and she was looking like she was ready to kill me. I didn't give a fuck though.

"I don't chill with you every night?" I pulled my phone out. And went through our text thread.

"We don't text and talk all day. I don't call you my baby girl?" I swear I wish I had a camera to show y'all Dreka's face. Her mouth was on the floor and she was stuck as shit.

"Dreka I asked you if you had a man and you told me no," pale ass patty finally spoke. I chuckled again and said.

"Well, she lied which was wrong on her end because she know my ass don't got'em all," I was about to say something else but I seen some shit in the back of his Magnum car that almost made me go buck wild.

"Yo' is that a overnight bag?!" I pointed and looked at Dreka. I swear to God I was about to break loose.

"What?! I mean wait a minute. Carter, Z is my friend and nothing-----,"

"Fuck that shit answer my muthafucking question?! You were coming or going?" I asked and I swear if she said she was coming I was about to go wild. I don't give a fuck call me nuts but I don't want to see or hear about Dreka spending----- Let me calm down and give her a chance to answer.

"Zamir I can not believe you right now, what is wrong with you?! I was going with him overnight," I pulled my gun out and when I tell y'all this nigga screamed louder and higher than Dreka I couldn't make this shit up. Bitch born nigga! I used the butt of my gun and broke his back window. I snatched her bag out and gave it to her.

"Dead this shit Dreka and get in my fucking truck," I was done here so I tucked my gun in my waist and walked back to my shit. I wasn't worried about her leaving with him because I swear I will shoot holes in that nigga car. I saw her grandma in the door smiling and laughing. Grams was wild but mad cool. Dreka's pops wasn't home thank God. I wasn't scared but I just didn't feel like dealing with him to. Like I told her to do, Dreka dismissed that nigga and walked to my truck. She was pissed off but I didn't care.

"Zamir Collins I cannot believe you! He never wants to see me again!" she yelled but I could tell she really didn't care. Hell I know I didn't.

"Good," I said as I pulled off into traffic.

"Where are we going?" she asked me.

"To Bucharest Grill on Livernois because I'm hungry

as hell. Then we going to my crib," I could feel her eyes go big and her mouth drop. I didn't even need to look at her. I had never taken a girl to my house. It just wasn't my thing but I don't know what came over me tonight. I just wanted her to come to my spot.

We got to Bucharest Grill and I was use to eating there because the food smelled good as fuck. They make the best fucking shawarmas and wraps in the city in my opinion. Shit was fire and the sauce they use tops it off. Dreka got her pretty chunky ass out and walked in with me. She was looking good as hell in some jean shorts. Her top had the word *Prince* on it and it was short and flared out. Them long thick mocha legs were out and she had on some purple Huaraches gym shoes.

I was happy she didn't have no weave in. Her long hair was in big ass curls all over her head. You know how the bitches with good hair can get away with that shit and it looks good. Them full ass lips had some sparkle gloss on them. Damn baby girl was just so fucking sexy. We placed our orders and sat down waiting on our food. I saw some niggas I knew and they spoke to me. Some nigga spoke to her and I looked at that nigga like I wanted to kill him. She laughed and told me he worked in a suite in Greenfield Plaza where she does hair.

"You know we talking about this shit when we get to your crib right?" she was looking at me and I looked above her head like I was trying to read the menu. I felt her soft ass hand grab mine all gentle and shit. I didn't mean to but I pulled away making her furrow her eyebrows. The lady called our food and I got up to go get it.

We drove and I let her control the radio. My mind was somewhere else. I don't know why I tripped like that when I saw Dreka with ol'boy. You know what let me stop lying, yes I do. I was feeling Dreka hard as fuck. Shit was wild how I wanted her and I don't mean just physically. Although given a chance I would tear that pussy up and eat it up. All shit that I have never done. I don't even trust bitches and here I was about to take her to my crib. What if she switches up on me? Turns out to be dirty as fuck and play me. I'm a big scary lookin' nigga but like I said earlier. I'm low key sensitive as fuck and don't play about my feelings. Shit was mad aggy. We had a minute from Detroit to Canton, so I just drove and kept over thinking shit.

***

"Wow Zamir, you have a nice condo. It's spacious as hell and nice for a guy to live here," she said as she looked around. I liked living here because it was quiet, by every store, restaurant, and entertainment. I had a two-bedroom condo. Both bedrooms were upstairs with two full bathrooms and a half downstairs. It was all beige carpet and the walls and staircase was a light brown. I had marble and cherry wood kitchen and chocolate brown and burgundy furniture. A nigga had good ass taste.

"Thanks, baby girl I appreciate that," I said to her as I sat our food and drinks on the dining room table. I watched Dreka take her shoes off and like always her nails matched her feet. A cute taupe color that looked good with her mocha skin. She had them sharp ass Cardi-B nails on but that shit looked mad sexy on her. I watched her finish walking around and sit her bag on my couch.

I let her pick something for us to watch and she picked the movie *Bebe's Kids.* We ate our food, laughed at the movie and talked a little. I told her about Cassidy and Alaric and her ass started laughing hard and wildin' out. She told me she wasn't going to say shit until Cassidy decided to tell her. We talked about Erin and Yatta's crazy asses. She told me about her visit with her mama. I thought that was cool how her pops looked out for her mama. Dreka really was close to her mama and it made me think about my own. That crazy fucked up ass lady. After eating and talking Dreka excused herself and grabbed her bag. I told her she can use whatever bathroom and she went upstairs.

This shit was cool as hell. I guess I did over think shit about her coming here. It was the same as when we were at her crib. Being around Dreka was a different vibe and I fucked with it heavy. She was like one of the homies but still girly with her shit. I decided to go upstairs and shower myself. I heard shit in the guest bathroom so I went to the bathroom in the master bedroom. I pulled out some boxers, hooping shorts, and a grey beater.

Turning on the shower I stepped my big ass in and let that hard shower hit me. I thought about Dreka while I got cleaned. The only love I know is from my sister. That shit was real and never switched up. I wasn't scared of that love. This shit right here was a lot and I knew for Dreka and my sake I needed to fall back.

I was done with my shower and dressed. After I put my deodorant on and put my dreads on top of my head and headed downstairs. I was cool until I saw Dreka sitting on my big ass couch with her wet hair all curly on top of her head. Her skin had no makeup or that sparkle shit on her lips. Her skin was flawless and I loved when she did no makeup because you got to really see her beauty. She had on some short ass pajama shorts with PINK all over it and matching shirt. We had stopped at the liquor store and got some junk food. She had it all on display on the table.

"You done made yourself at home huh?" I joked with her. Believe it or not, I smiled big as fuck whenever I was with Dreka. I joked, laughed and was silly with her. I was myself with my sister but I was more in big brother mode with her.

"I sure did since I'm here against my will," she said and we both started laughing. I sat down and picked up my pack of Twizzlers. She was eating on her Sour Patch candy with her FUJI water.

"How old are you again sitting here watching Family Guy?!" I teased her. She smacked them pretty full lips and said.

"I knowww you not talking. I saw on your history that you were watching Dragon Ball Z! Yo' ass a big kid nigga," she started laughing and teasing. I put my candy down and yanked her ass by me. I started tickling and fucking up her hair.

"Ahh! Zamir stop punk!" she screamed while laughing hard as hell. I was talking shit while making her laugh hard.

"Ugh nigga, yo' ass all slobbing!" I cracked up as she slobbed and snorted from laughing hard.

"Yo' you sound like a farm animal!" I was dead ass cracking up and she started punching me while laughing.

"Shut up don't talk about me! I do that if I laugh to hard punk ass!" we laughed together and kept playing.

"Zamir can I ask you something?" she asked me as we got our shit together. She was still sitting close as hell to me but I low key didn't want her to move.

"What's up baby girl?" she cleared her throat and her eyes met with mine.

"Are you feelin' me as more than friends?" she caught me off guard when she asked that. Before I could respond my natural instincts kicked in making me say some foul shit.

"Hell naw. Dreka I don't do feelings and shit with bitches," my oversize stupid ass blurted out. The look she gave me said it all, she looked off, chuckled and said.

"Wow, I'm sorry I asked," putting her candy on the table she stood up and walked upstairs. I watched her go and heard the second bedroom door close.

Fuck! I said to myself. I swear I didn't mean to say that shit. I was used to bitches asking me that all the time and that's what my response was. Sometimes I don't answer at all and just drop they asses. But Dreka was different and I knew it. Fuck it, it was this or lose her. I got up and went upstairs. In front of the door, I took a deep breath and knocked. I heard her say come in and I slowly opened the door. When I closed it and walked over to the bed she was sitting with her phone in her hand. I had a 45-inch in this room with cable because sometimes Cassidy would stay the night. I sat on the side where she was at and rubbed my hand over my face.

"I ain't good at this shit Dreka. I don't do relationships, romance, caking and shit," I shook my head.

"It ain't me at all. My mama fucked me all up as far as how I look at bi—women. I don't trust and truth be told. I'm sensitive as hell and don't play about my feelings," I paused a little and finally looked at her in the eyes.

"Baby girl I will kill yo' ass if you were to play me and that's real shit. Women plot, use and play a lot of games. Ain't no real shit out here in 2018 and I don't have time for that. But what I feel for you is making me feel different. I know when I saw you with ol'boy I wanted to fuck you and him up. It's like you mine but I know you not mine. Shit weird but that's how I feel." She climbed out the bed and sat next to me. When she took my hand in hers and enter locked our fingers. This time I didn't pull away. Her touch actually felt good as hell. Looking at me she said.

"Zamir do you want me to be yours? Be honest." Her soft voice asked me. I looked straight ahead and then back at her.

"Honestly I don't wanna fuck shit up. I like you in my life Dreka and I love different from any other nigga that you probably will ever be with. Even though I have never did this before I know I can love hard. Look how I love my sister. I just never met a girl that I wanted to do that with. Ya, feel me?"

"I do and I understand but Zamir if we stay friends then I am going to do me like I know you are going to do you," I got mad when she said that shit.

"Don't say that shit to me Dreka. You my baby girl and I don't want to hear that shit," since we were being honest I might as well keep the shit up.

"So what do we do?" she asked me and I looked at her hand in mine. The shit felt right and looked good as hell. I thought about the person she was, all our years of chilling together. Her falling asleep next to me and me kissing her on the forehead and leaving her crib. I thought about all our talks and how she doesn't judge. I thought about how she makes me drop my guard without even trying. And finally, I thought about her with ol'boy. Naw, that shit ain't gone fly. I cleared my throat and like a true bitch. My heart was beating fast and my hands were getting sweaty.

"Be my girl Dreka," I said to her and she gave me a big sexy smile.

"Ok, Zamir. I'll be your girl but only if you promise to treat me right and not play me either," I smiled at her.

"I got you baby girl," I used my finger to grab her chin and brought her in for a kiss. Our first fucking kiss! Her lips touched mine and damn they were as soft as I imagined. When I felt her slip her tongue in my mouth I had no idea what to do. I had never tongue kissed before. She pulled away and looked at me with a smirk.

"Follow my lead," her sweet soft voice said. I agreed and this time when she kissed me I moved the same paced she did.

Our tongues touched and massaged each other. That shit was fucking live. I was getting hard as fuck and before you knew it. I was mastering that shit. I was biting and sucking on her juicy ass bottom lip. My lips were juicy to so she was having a field day on my lips. I pulled her on my lap so she could straddle me. Standing up with her in my arms and us still kissing I walked us to my room. I needed my California King bed for the way I wanted to fuck Dreka juicy chunky ass. Laying her on my fluffy ass black comforter she looked good as fuck looking at me biting her lip.

I stood between her legs and took my beater off. I grabbed a Magnum in my side drawer. Don't judge me but I had a dresser full of them. I'd grab about three a day and put them in my wallet. Looking at Dreka had my dick hard as fuck. I dropped my boxers and shorts freeing that muthafucka. Her eyes bugged out and she looked at me hesitant. I smirked and put the condom on the bed. I heard shit about tall thick niggas like myself weren't packing. Well God showed me favor because I had a thick, brown ten-inch savage.

I leaned forward in her face and kissed the fuck out of her. That tongue shit was my new thang. I loved that shit and only wanted to do it with her so I hope she was cool with it. I could see myself wanting to shove my tongue down her mouth every time I see her after this. I felt her take my tie out my dreads letting them fall. I pulled her shirt over her head and was happy she didn't have a bra on. Dreka had some nice ass D-cup titties with big light brown nipples. I attacked the fuck out of them. I licked, kissed, sucked and when I saw she liked that ruff shit. I bit down on her nipples a little. I knew she was going to have at least one hickey on each titty.

She was moaning all in my ear driving my ass wild. I kissed her some more and slipped my hand in her shorts. She was bald and wet ass fuck. Dreka's pussy lips were fat ass fuck and when I rubbed her clit she hissed like a snake. I went to licking and sucking on her neck as I slid a finger in her pussy. That muthafucker was tight as fuck. I couldn't fuckin' believe it I was so close to asking her was she a virgin. Her walls felt soft and wet as fuck. Looking at her throw her head back, biting her bottom lip and close her eyes. I smiled to myself because Dreka was in full ecstasy and I hadn't even dicked her down yet.

"Open them eyes Dreka," she did as I said and I almost shot my kids all on my ceiling from looking at her sexy ass face. I slid one more finger in her and started working them slowly and I talked.

"I don't want no problems out of you a'ight. You got a crazy, short-fused, jealous, possessive ass nigga. I don't wanna show out but I swear I will if you test me. All this shit is new but I'm willing to try. You down?" my voice was deep and low and it must have been turning her on because she was getting wetter.

"Ssss yes, Zamir. I'm down baby ooo my goodness I'm gonna cum," I curved my fingers and knocked on that spot. Looking down at Dreka's pussy, she had squirted all on my hand. That shit was hot as fuck. Her back was arched and her naked ass body was looking good as fuck. I wanted to do another first tonight.

I got up and stood between her legs again. I spread her legs and bent them back far. I thought I was hurting her but this fucking girl blew me the fuck away. She took each leg and put it behind her arms. The shit made me want to take a picture of it. I had no idea what I was doing because I had never done it before. But I do know that the clit was the shit to focus on and since it was her second set of lips. I was just going to tongue kiss, lick and kiss on that fat cat.

I kneeled down, licked my lips and dove in head first. Dreka pussy tasted as good as it looked. My face between them fat lips was turning me on. I started moving my head in slow circles, her juices was making me make a lot of noise and her taste was making me fucking moan. Some shit I don't fucking do. I must have been doing a good job because she was yelling shit and bunching my dreads in her hand.

"Oh, my God Zamir mmmhmm," I went buck on her shit making her back arch but her still kept them legs behind her. Her clit was fat and when I had that bitch in my mouth Dreka went crazy. I was feeling myself now so I reached up and put both my hands up around her neck. Still eating her good I choked her a little and like a true fucking freak, she loved that shit. I made her come twice and I slurped that shit all up making her body shake. I kissed her sexy ass stomach, them hot ass stretch marks, her full ass titties and finally her first set of lips.

"Fuck baby that was so fucking good," she said against my lips.

"I can tell. You sound good as fuck moaning my name," I picked the condom up, opened it and put it on. I was ready to fuck and if I didn't then my dick was going to dip on me. Dreka pushed me back down on the bed. She started kissing me and climbing on top of me. I pulled away and said.

"Don't ride my shit if you can't ride right," she smacked her lips while lifting up.

When she put that warm tight pussy on my dick I almost ran out the room and hid. Her shit was so tight. I was too thick for her tight walls so she had to slide down slow as fuck. Them sexy ass titties and her face was too much to look at but I couldn't bitch up and close my eyes. Once I was in she leaned forward and kissed me again. I grabbed the back of my head and tried to swallow her pretty ass. She slowly started going up and down on my dick. Fuck me for life. I knew right then and there that I wanted Dreka forever. She was it for me and that was just fucking that. Gorgeous, cool as fuck, smart, not a thot and good pussy that feels and taste amazing. That's all I needed, this was my wife right here.

"Fuck Zamir. Arghhh baby yo' dick so fucking thick!" she was bouncing like a porno hoe now and I was here for tha shit! She felt good as fuck and I could hear loud water slapping telling me she was cummin'. When she slowed down I wasn't having that. With her still, on top of me, I put each of her legs in the crook of my arm. My big ass hands were on her back and I started lifting her slamming here up and down on my dick. Any of you BBW's reading this that got a nigga who can't lift you like this shouldn't be yo' nigga. You gotta get you a nigga that lifts you like you a size three.

"WHAT! THE! FUCK! ZAMIRRRR! SHIT!" Dreka was yelling my name making my walls shake and my ego grow.

"Give me all of that pussy bitch! You my fuckin' bitch now! Mmmhmm! Whose pussy is this Dreka? Tell daddy," I was still bouncing her while her arms were holding her up.

"Ahhh shit! It's yours Zamir. Shit, it's all yours!" That did it for me I came hard as fuck in the condom. Dreka squirted all on my chest and that shit turned me on. I let her legs go and we both were breathing hard. Dreka fell backwards while still on top of me. I sat up and grabbed her neck pulling her up. Tonguing her down slow and sweet. I looked at her pretty ass face. We both were sweating and her pretty ass hair was pressed against her face.

"This shit right here is locked in forever. I ain't gone

find nothing like this again," I told her looking her in her eyes. We were only twenty-two, but I didn't give a fuck. I was being honest and I hope she was down.

"I'm cool with that Zamir. This is something I been wanting for a while. But you should know I don't play either. I got jealous ways and I sure can show my ass about you. So behave yourself as long as you're my nigga," This bitch was turning me the fuck on talking like that. I kissed her again before I asked her.

"You mine Dreka?" I just loved hearing the shit out loud. Her pretty ass smiled and nodded her head.

"You mine Zamir?" I bit my lip and nodded my head. Kissing her again I wanted some more and clearly, she did too. I fucked her again doggy style and her ass was going buck wild squirting all on my bed. We went at it so much that I fucking lost count. When I woke up the next morning, there were six condom wrappers on the floor.

***

"I hate I gotta go to work," Dreka said as she was about to get out my truck. I was dropping her off at her job. She had some hair appointments to do today.

"Don't trip, you spending the night with me again," I bit my lip looking at her. Her cute ass blushed and smiled. She leaned over and gave me a kiss.

"What time you get off again?" I asked her that just fucking with her. I knew she told me to come back and get her at three o' clock.

"Zamir don't play bae. I said three, please don't leave me stranded," I kissed her again and squeezed her booty.

"I got you baby girl I would never leave you stranded," we kissed again and I watched her pretty ass walk in to the building.

I pulled off on my way to open up the boxing gym. I decided to stop at Sunshine liquor store on Lyndon. I needed some rellos and a cranberry juice. Walking in I gave a bum who was begging a five-dollar bill. This was one of my liquor stores and I was cool with the owner. I spoke and laughed it up for a minute. Paying for my juice and rellos I walked out back into the Detroit heat. When I got to my truck a white Charger was parked next to it and some fat ass nigga was eating some Wendys. I already knew this was the same suit that Yatta was talking about. I shook my head and walked towards my truck. He had that same badge and gun on display like Yatta described.

"Have a good day Mr. Collins," he said as he kept eating his sandwich. I started to say some smart shit but I declined to. I just got in my car, started it up and pulled off. Looking in my rear-view mirror he still was sitting on the hood of his car eating. I pulled my burner phone out and texted my day ones and Lonell's burner and told them that suit got to me too. Putting the phone back in my pocket. I just hoped this shit was not about to catch up to us. Not now, and I finally got my baby girl on my team.

<u>Erin</u>

"So you excited about your date tomorrow? He's fine as hell girl," I was at work messing with Cassidy. Her new guy came up and brought her some flowers. He was fine as hell, a little on the slim side but still fine. I can tell she liked him but not as much as she liked Alaric. I couldn't stand his ass for what he did to her.

"I am girl. Jamil is sweet, fine and a gentleman," she responded while counting down one of her registers. I had just clocked out because I had to go meet my dad's friend who wanted to pay me to imitate some art for his store.

"Why do I feel like there's a 'but' about to come out your mouth?" I asked looking at her with a smirk and my eyebrow arched. She started shaking her head smiling.

"You make me sick, ya know that. You know what I'm about to say," we both laughed.

"It's ok to miss Alaric boo. Your fucking human and y'all had a mad ass vibe. That baby would have been gorgeous as hell," I smiled teasing her. She playfully shoved me and we laughed.

"Why do we do this? We will have a nice, easy going guy. What the fuck we need and have been asking for. Yet, the guy who is fine, good dick but comes with a shit load of problems. We seem to can't shake for shit," Cassidy did a loud sign and all I could do was agree.

"Hayden has been texting and calling me. He fine as fuck has a good future ahead of him and has a nice ass family. I know we would be good together and have a good life. But, Kenyatta just stays on my mind and heart," I couldn't help but smile big when I said his name and Cassidy noticed to.

"*Kenyatta!* Oh, were on government name basis now!

I love it and it's about time. I knew it when he took you out
the day after his party. He really is a good dude just got some
hood ways in him. But what bitch don't like that shit," me
and her laughed and high fived each other. She was right,
Kenyatta was a good dude. I liked him and we had been
spending some time together over the last three weeks. I was
loving it even though he still gave me butterflies and made
me nervous. He was just so fine, aggressive and blunt which
was new to me. Me and Cassidy kept talking and laughing
when I saw Alaric walk in the store.

"Cassidy, Alaric just walked it," I said that shit to her
and her posture and face changed.

"He's alone and looking around. Oh, shit bitch he is
coming this way," Cassidy closed register drawer and walked
from behind the counter. I wasn't moving because if he was
about to be on some bullshit with my best friend. I was going
to hit his ass in the head with the stapler sitting on the
counter.

"What are you doing here Alaric? Shopping for
another bitch again?" I did a low laugh but chilled when I
saw Alaric's face. He looked so sad and pathetic. His dreads
were all down and his facial hair was a little thicker. He had
on some True Religion jean shorts and a basic white t-shirt.
Like always he was rocking some Jordan Retro Orange. He
still looked good just effortless. Holy fuck, not pimp Alaric?!
Not keep a bitch on her knees begging and pleading Alaric!?
Lord Jesus my best friend must have some gold between her
legs.

"Cassidy, can we please talk, please? No games or all
the extra shit. I just wanna holla at you for a second,"
Cassidy was shaking her head before he could even finish his
sentence.

"Alaric you did this shit. All you had to do was be
real with me and tell me what was up. You had me thinking
we were on some us shit. When really you were all for you!
Now you want to be in my face after I don't react the way
most bitches you fuck with do? Naw, I'm good on you for

real," I looked at Cassidy then at Alaric. How fucking awkward was it to be right here in the middle. Part of me wanted to move but I was fucking stuck. I couldn't believe Alaric Bell was begging and looking like a sad puppy dog.

"I'm not even on that shit man on some real shit just hear me out," he walked closer to her.

"I miss you Cass love," *Cass love?!* I thought to myself. I was about to cry for him. Part of me wanted to shake Cassidy and tell her to stop being hard. But I understood where she was coming from. Still, who doesn't like a begging pleading nigga who thought his shit never stank!

"I don't care Alaric, you hurt me and played me. We're done so please leave," When she said that Alaric looked so defeated. He looked at her for a minute like he was searching for something. Cassidy was looking like she wanted to cry and with that Alaric turned around and walked out. I was so stunned. I walked around the counter and hugged my best friend. Two of our co-workers watched the shit like a movie and thank God it was customers in the store but they were at the other end not paying attention.

"It's ok Cassidy boo. You did what's best for you but I just want you to make sure this is what you want. I saw your face and his face and I think now that his guard is down yours is up strong. Just take some time and think about it," she wiped her face and nodded her head. I kissed my best friend on the cheek and smiled at her.

"Erin?" We both turned around and I saw my half-brother Jamie walk towards us smiling.

"Oh, hi Jamie," I hugged him and introduced him and Cassidy.

"You all the way at Fairlane shopping?" I asked him because he lived in Lansing and they had a pluther of shopping choices to choose from.

"I had a small case at Downtown Courthouse. I'm only an intern so it was all coffee runs but still," he smiled and responded.

"You want to go to the food court and get something to eat?" he asked me and I looked at my phone and realized I had a little over an hour to spare. I hugged Cassidy and told her if she needed me for anything to call me.

Jamie and I walked out into the mall. Forever 21 was on the third floor along with the food court. We had to walk to the opposite end though. Me and Jamie talked a little about him in interning for a law office where he lives. He really loved it and seem to have a deep passion for it. I told him about my painting and drawing. How I have always loved it and one day I will be able to live off my drawings and paintings. They will be in a museum and some of the world's most prestigious auctions.

He was really supportive and sweet about it. We got to the food court and decided to eat Sbarro's pizza. I only could eat one slice of meat lovers and be full ass shit. Jamie ordered a slice and a salad. We grabbed our tray of food and sat down at a booth. He sat across from me in a chair. Fairlane mall wasn't empty today. I cracked up when girls walked by and stared at Jamie. Swear these bitches be so outta line. Even though he was my brother they didn't know that shit. Then they get mad when a chick like me slaps their ass for being rude.

"So, how was it growing up with our mother?" I asked him while picking up my slice of pizza. Jamie laughed and shook his head.

"She is tuff as nails. Always wanted me to be something great, make good grades, dress respectful and make friends with people who can open doors for you," we both shook our heads and laugh. It's a damn shame me and my mother were in the same state and she had nothing to do with raising me. I mean, who the fuck does that shit?!

"Sounds like her. I see you rebelling today?" I said pointing to his outfit. It wasn't casual wear at all. He had on a Nike tracksuit with a black beater under the jacket and some red high-top Nike's on his feet.

"I'm a grown ass man now so I just tell her to chill on

the noise," we both laughed. Jamie was cool as hell so far. Nothing like I assumed him to be.

"I'm sorry she wasn't there for you like she was supposed to be. I hope you won't let that stand in the way of us developing a bond," I smiled at Jamie and shook my head.

"I wouldn't do that. I mean you're here, making an effort to get to know me. I appreciate that," he was about to say something but in a flash, Jamie was yanked out of his chair on to the floor. I looked at him and then up at Yatta mean ass face.

"Yo' who the fuck is this dork ass nigga you smiling at?!" I jumped up to help Jamie up but Yatta blocked me.

"Yatta that's my half brother Jamie! Move!" I pushed him and helped Jamie stand up.

"I am so sorry Jamie. This is my crazy ass friend Yatta," I looked at him with a snarled look. Yatta still was looking mean as fuck as he looked at me and Jamie.

"My bad G I thought you was trying to push up on my girl," he said to Jamie but still looking at me. Jamie fixed his clothes and shook Yatta's hand.

"It's all good man. I know how it looks because I have never been around. Our mother is to thank for that," he tried to make a joke but I was still so embarrassed and mad that I didn't even say shit. Yatta still was giving me his stank ass look.

"Well, baby sis I gotta get going. I'll call you later and maybe we can have dinner with mama," I smiled at Jamie and agreed. We hugged, he gave Yatta another handshake and walked off. I turned and looked at Yatta. Nosey ass people were looking at us waiting to see what was going to happen. This fool sat down and started eating my pizza like nothing happened.

"Yatta, you can not just pop up and behave that way. You completely violated my brother instead of you just introducing yourself and ask who he was," I sat in the seat Jamie was in. Yatta kept eating as if I wasn't talking to him.

"Um, excuse me. You don't hear me talking to you?"

I asked getting annoyed. I was about to walk away from his rude ass.

"I don't know who the fuck you talking to because I specifically told you to call me Kenyatta. Yatta is for niggas and these bitches. Not my fucking woman," he didn't even look at me as he talked. He was going to work on my pizza. Ass! I couldn't help but admire how fucking sexy he looked though. He had on some jeans, a royal blue Polo that fitted his frame nice. That iced out 'Yatta' chain and some Lebron Agimat's on his feet. He had them sexy ass dreads half up and half down. Damn, he was so fine and them lips. Mm! Them lips were lookin' fuckin' right. I needed to calm my hot ass down.

"Kenyatta," he looked up at me and licked his lips.

"Yes, cutie pie?" my damn heart skipped a beat.

"You can't behave like that," that's all I fucking had. He was looking so good I forgot all about my speech I had.

"I do what the fuck I want. When I see that gorgeous ass smile in another niggas face I gotta react baby," he looked on the side of me and shook his head.

"What is that called that your wearing?" I looked at my outfit and then back at him. He had killed my pizza and now he was wiping his hands and drinking my Sprite.

"A romper. Why?" I asked him looking confused. I was regular with a black romper on. Some silver Michael Kors flip flops on and my curly hair in two high ponytails. My nails and feet were done in pink and white.

"You don't think I look cute today?" I asked smiling big at him. He smiled back and I almost fell out my chair. His teeth were so white and straight and that dip on the top of his lip was hot.

"I think you look sexy as fuck. It's a little short and I saw that booty jiggle when you got up but you still look good as hell. We gotta get you some more of them romper thangs," he smirked and looked at me. I had to turn away because I was getting nervous.

"Erin," ugh, there he goes calling my name and

telling me to look at him. I turned and looked in his eyes and he smiled.

"That's better. What'chu about to do?" I told him I was about to go to meet with my dad friend about some drawings. Then he asked me about my brother and I told him that he wanted a relationship with me. He doesn't agree how our mama kept us apart. Kenyatta was happy for me and told me he hoped it all worked out.

"Drop your car at your house and let me take you to your art meeting. I want you with me today. Cool?" I smiled and nodded my head.

"Where my kiss at? You that pissed because I knocked Norbit on his ass?" I know I was wrong but I couldn't help but laugh at him calling Jamie Norbit. He was a little nerdy but he didn't look like Norbit. Kenyatta was laughing too.

"Don't be talking about my brother, ass," he held his chain flat in his chest and leaned forward. I met him halfway and we kissed. His lips were soft and always wet which I loved. Our first time kissing was after our date at Andiamo. He was so sweet and we had a nice ass time eating and talking. We talked about high school days, my time in New York, his son and when he went away to jail. He didn't get into details but we talked about what he learned and how he didn't want to end up back there.

"Soft ass fucking lips you got. Come on," we both got up. I noticed he had some bags from Macy's and 4MEN clothing store.

He carried his bags in one hand and he grabbed my hand with his free one. The butterflies were going wild in my belly. It had always been like this whenever I was around him. Its just now we touch and talk more. We kiss and are a little more intimate now. Speaking of intimate, I still haven't told him I was a virgin. I don't know I was just scared that he would run away if I told him. The way Kenyatta is and what he is used to, I know I can't compete with that. The only thing I have done was kiss had had my pussy licked. I was conflicted, but I know sooner or later I would have to tell him. It's only so long before he gets bored with this no sex thing.

Kenyatta walked me to my Kia and I got in and waited for him to get to his truck and follow me. I played *Sevyn Streeter Girl Disrupted* album and pulled off. I thought about my brother and my mama. I hadn't told my dad about my mama's visit with Jamie. I didn't want my dad to feel any type of way about me getting to know Jamie. I mean he is the product of my mama cheating on him. But part of me appreciated Jamie for wanting a relationship with me. Then I thought about this sexy ass nigga driving behind me. Kenyatta was becoming apart of my life and I was low key loving it. I just didn't want drama with his stupid ass baby mama. Plus, was I ready to play step-mama to his baby. See this is what I always do, over think shit. I just needed to chill and enjoy my young life. Right?

***

"So you want her to do the paint the picture that a customer orders. You want her to supply her own art supplies and bring the paintings to you which is gas she would be using all for four hundred dollars a painting? Get the fuck outta here my nigga," I looked at Kenyatta with big eyes as he talked to my dad's friend Rowland like he wasn't older than us. We were in Rowland store in Royal Oak.

"I'm sorry, who are you again?" Rowland pointed at Kenyatta and asked. He had a thick Arabic accent.

"I'm her fuckin' everything my nigga and I'm also the one telling you that you not about to play her. You get what, a little over four-grand each painting. Naw. She need at least half each painting and you supply her art supplies. You sell imitation art and I can bet my left ball that you ain't finding a better painter then her," I looked at Rowland and he looked at Yatta.

"Deal, but only because I know her father and he is an excellent artist," I smiled and kissed Yatta on his cheek.

"Thank you, Kenyatta. This money is really going to

help," I smiled at him and said.

"You welcome cutie pie but don't kiss me on my cheek like I'm one of them little ass dogs bitches keep in their purse. I want lips on lips baby," he pulled me over to him and kissed me. I loved how our tongues filled when they touched.

His breath was always on point and did I mention how I love his aggressiveness. The shit was so sexy. We kissed until we heard Rowland clear his throat. I know my face was red as hell. Rowland gave me the art supplies and told me in two weeks I needed to have Vincent Van Gogh Starry Night and Claude Monet Water Lilies done. He gave me two 8x10 colored pictures of both paintings. It was going to be so easy to do this and the extra money would help me out. Plus my job at Forever 21 would help. I wanted to get my own place and pay my own car note. My dad loved me staying with him but I was ready for my own space. He also didn't mind paying my car note but I needed to act like an adult.

"So where to now? I have nothing else I need to do," I asked Kenyatta as he opened the door for me. He walked around to his side and got in.

"You coming with me to the tattoo and piercing shop I work at. Well one of them. Gallery Tattoos on seven mile," I nodded my head and turned the radio on. Kenyatta was playing Peezy album and I hit the radio button. He laughed.

"You don't like Detroit rappers?" He asked me while I turned the radio to 105.9 radio station.

"Not really, they sound the same. I like Big Sean though," he laughed and waved me off.

"I'm gone change that shit. We gotta put'chu on some Babyface Ray, Peezy or at least some Icewear Vezzo!" He was all geeked up telling me these people names like I'm supposed to know who they were.

"I fucks with this old school you just put on also." He said and I saw an aux cord sticking out his radio. I pulled my phone out and plugged it in.

"Oh Lord, that means you about to play some girly ass music," his smart-ass said and I laughed because he was right.

"Shut up I been loving *Sevyn Streeter* a lot lately she's a good artist" he shook his head and let me do my thing. I played her song Before I do. Don't talk about, me but I purposely wanted him to hear this song. I thought it fitted me and him to the T.

I heard about, you and your other situation
Through word of mouth
They made it seem so complicated
Is it over now?
Or did you just say it 'cause you're anxious?
To get closer now
'Cause I want you to be, all over me

I was jamming to her and the lyrics. Kenyatta let me turn it up as loud as I wanted. I could feel him stealing glances at me but I ignored him and kept singing to the words.

Truthfully (Truthfully)
Honestly (Honestly)
I need, I need, I need to believe
I wanna let go, but I don't really know
I heard you got a girlfriend
Say it ain't so, you ain't on the low
I don't think I could handle it
I wanna go, to another level, with you
But before I do
I wanna know before I go there with you
Oh yeah, so tell me you're through
I need to know before I go there with you

I was jamming and he reached over and turned my song down. That broke me out of my trance and singing.

"That's how you feel Erin?" I looked at him because he called me by my real name which was rare. He had a serious expression on his face. He looked from me to the road and waited for me to answer.

"In a way, it is Kenyatta I do. You have a baby with Cleo and plus I'm—," I caught myself because I was about to slip and say I was a virgin. Thank God he didn't catch it. We got off the freeway and he pulled over down a random block.

"Erin, I swear to you nothing is going on with me and Cleo. We fucked and made my son but that's all. I was leaving a hype ass party drunk and faded off a pill I popped. I wasn't thinking when I showed up at her crib and we fucked unprotected. I swear to God me and that girl ain't never been shit but on some fucking level," he grabbed my hand and kissed it.

"I know during high school and even after you thought I was never feeling you. But that shit ain't true Erin. I just knew you were into your art and wanted big things outside of the hood. I used to watch you daydream and draw random things around the school. That shit made you stand out in a good way and a nigga like me thought you didn't need my ass in your life. So, I was stuck fucking with bitches like Cleo's rat ass. But shit different now and I believe I deserve you and you deserve me. On some real G shit, a'ight," I was blown away with what Kenyatta had just said to me. I always thought he preferred Cleo over me. She was advanced and more popular than I was. I thought I was too weird or too much of a nerd for him. I guess I was wrong. I smiled at him and rubbed the side of his face.

"A'ight baby," he leaned over and kissed my ass so deep I swear my sandals popped off my feet. He picked my phone up and went to my Spotify app.

"We turning your damn song off because you don't need nothing stopping you from going to the next level with me," he took a second and when he played his song choice I laughed and shook my head.

Girl if I told you I love you
That doesn't mean that I don't care, oooh
And when I tell you I need you
Don't you think that I'll never be there, ooooh
Baby, I'm so tired of the way you turn my words into

Deception and lies
Don't misunderstand me when I try to speak my mind
I'm only saying what's in my heart
Cupid doesn't lie
But you won't know unless you give it a try
Oh baby, true love
won't lie but we won't know unless we give it a try
give it a try

112 Cupid song played and I blushed when he sung the words to me. He had it up loud and knew every word. He tried it hard as fuck! I know I was cheesing like a damn creep but I couldn't help it. This was so sweet and from now on I was going to play this song so much when I paint or take a shower.

Girl when I ask you to trust me
That doesn't mean that I'm gonna cheat on you
Cuz I'm gonna never do anything to hurt you
Or mislead you, I love you

He held my hand in his lap the whole time until we got to his job. I felt all gitty in the inside after what he told me and the song he played. He opened my door and grabbed my hand to help me out his big ass truck. I loved walking around with Yatta in the city. He had so much swag that sat him apart from the typical Detroit guy. I felt exclusive being with him and almost untouchable. We walked in the shop and there was loud music playing and a bunch of tattoos all on the walls. Some girls were in there and obviously part of his fan club because they looked at me like they wanted to fight.

"What's poppin' Foxx, Dread Head," I watched as Kenyatta spoke to all the tattoo artists. Some girl was in the corner with her sidekick whispering shit. Yatta looked at me licking his sexy ass lips.

"This my girl Erin y'all. Erin this the annoying ass crew," he told me as I smiled and spoke to everyone. The guys showed him some more love.

"God damn nigga, she fine as hell. You got some sisters?" One of the guys asked me.

"Naw nigga, she ain't got no sisters and quit fuckin' drooling all over my girl," Kenyatta joked as we walked back to what I assume was his room.

"Yatta, when you gone re-pierce my clit again?" I looked up at this bitch with red hair funky ass face. She was sucking on a cherry sucker and looking at him like she wanted to drop on her knees.

"Bitch don't be disrespectful and you see my girl right here. And I ain't piercing that bullshit no more. Even with gloves on I still couldn't get the smell out my hands. Ebola ass pussy," I as well as his co-workers laughed our asses off. The chick mouth hung open and she stomped off. Walking in Kenyatta's room he closed the door as I looked around at his working space. He had tattoo drawings on one of the walls. He was really good and on the other wall were pictures of him and his clients showing off their tattoos he did.

"Oh my goodness. When did you meet these people?" I smiled pointing at the pictures and looking at him. He had pictures with The Game, Chris Brown, Lil Wayne, and Tyga. Kenyatta walked over where I was.

"Oh shit, that was around winter and springtime. They didn't come together it was at separate times," I smiled at him because that was great exposure for him.

"I'm proud of you Kenyatta. This is going to be so good when you open your own shop," he smiled back at me. Sexy ass.

"So, is Chris Brown tall and as dreamy as he look on TV?" he smacked his lips and playfully nudged my head.

"You want me to cut yo' pretty ass face up with this tattoo gun?" he asked making me and him laugh.

"Come here," I looked at him and shook my head fast as hell.

"No! You are not about to ink me, Kenyatta," he stood up and pulled me to his chair.

"I ain't about to ink you. You gone let me pierce that pretty ass belly button that I know you have," when he said that I blushed and got scared. I nodded my head and he kissed me. Pulling away be bit his bottom lip and said.

"I got you cutie pie, you in the best hands," I smiled and nodded my head. He laid me down on the chair and reclined it back some. My romper buttoned up in the front so while he set up and turned the radio on. I unbuttoned it all the way to my belly button. I was so happy I decided to wear my nude lace bra and matching thong.

"Damn Erin," his reaction was funny when he turned around and saw my romper open. I had to think of something else to hold my laugh in.
"I know you have seen your share of bitches in bras," I said joking with him. He licked his sexy lips.

"I have but this shit right here," he pointed to my body. "This shit is fucking art. Anytime yo' artistic ass needs inspiration you should just look in the mirror," I blushed when he said that and covered my face up. He sat down on his stool and pulled my hands down.

"Stop covering up that pretty ass face baby," he kissed me again and I was at a lost of words. I watched him clean my belly button. He counted to three and pierced me on two. I almost pissed on myself the sharp pain I felt. I opened my eyes and he was done and telling me how to take care of it. He gave me a mirror so I could see it and I fell in love.

"Oh my God Kenyatta I love it. Thank you, this shit is hot," I looked at him beaming.

"I told yo ass that shit was gonna be fire. That'll be one President Grant, my baby," he held his hand out smiling. I laughed and gave his ass a high fived and buttoned my romper back up.

"I like how you smile and joke a lot. It's so many guys who walk around looking like they wanna kill the world. But you smile and joke around making people around you do the same," I told him as I got up.

"I'm always smiling and showing off these pretty whites but I ain't shit nice baby. I'm nice to you, my family and my two niggas. I'm cordial with the rest of the world until I lose or until somebody pisses me off," I looked at him confused.

"What do you mean lose?" I asked while he was cleaning up.

"Like if I lose anything. If I was to lose my son because of his mama being stupid. Or if I was to lose you to that nigga Hayden or anybody else. Shit wouldn't be good," I was looking at him as he talked and he was dead ass serious.

"Kenyatta not everyone wins. The way life is set up sometimes you're going to take a loss babe," he shook his head at me.

"See you're confused. Taking a loss that I can bounce back from is different. I can handle that. But some shit that's mine or some shit I really want. I don't take no for an answer and I don't ever fucking lose," I had to test what he was saying.

"So, if Cleo decided to move out of state and she took K.J.," he looked at me with his nose turned up.

"I'd kill that hoe and she knows it. Look, Erin, just know that I have a short ass temper and I don't like to lose. If yo pretty ass wouldn't have came around to being my girl then we would have a problem." See there he goes again with that title.

"To be fair Kenyatta I'm not your girl. I haven't been properly asked and I told you I didn't want to deal with Cleo's drama," he walked over to me and yanked my ass hard as hell to him.

"You not fucking single Erin and if you be out in these streets like you are. You gone see a whole other side of me," the look he gave me was almost deranged but still calm. He pecked my lips, smiled big and said.

"I'm hungry as hell. Let's get some Micky D's Coney Island and head to my crib," he pulled out his phone and I stood there looking stuck. Oh Lord please don't let me have a crazy nigga on my hands.

***

"Yo' ass eat like a football team. I can't believe you

ate all that damn food. "I laughed at Kenyatta teasing me. We ordered our food and brought it back to his nice ass apartment downtown. I ordered two Coney dogs and some wingdings. Kenyatta ordered a chicken pita and some chili cheese fries.

"Shut up, don't talk about me when yo'ass is just as greedy," I helped him clean up the kitchen counter. We sat on his bar stools and ate on his kitchen isle. Kenyatta had a nice ass two-bedroom apartment on the top floor. He showed me Alaric's door that was three down from him. His color scheme was grey, white and midnight blue. Very masculine in my opinion.

"Next time we leaving that shit alone and I'm cooking for you," my head shot up when he said that.

"You can cook?" he laughed at my response.

"Damn girl, give a nigga some credit. Yea I can cook baby and I would love to cook for yo' ass. Come on," he grabbed my hand and we walked to his bedroom. My heart was beating fast as fuck. It was a little after nine and I can't imagine us eating, chilling and him taking me home late as hell. *Oh boy, are you ready for this Erin?* I asked myself.

"You got a movie you want to watch. If I pick you know I'm picking some G shit," he passed me the remote. I picked it up and went to his Netflix app. I hurried up and picked *Katt Williams* new stand-up. I haven't saw it yet and I'm hoping Kenyatta hasn't either.

"Good choice baby. I ain't got a chance to watch it yet," I watched him take off his clothes and leave his boxers on. He put them in the hamper and walked over to his dresser drawer to pull out a beater.

"Here you go, baby. If you want to get out of your clothes," I smiled and grabbed it to put it on.

Well, I guess I'm staying the night. I undressed and I thought he would be trying to get a peek in but he was busy in his phone. I kept my bra and thong on and put the beater on. He put his phone down and pulled the covers back. I got in his big ass king size bed and damn it was soft as fuck. He had blue cotton sheets and a soft ass blue and black comforter on his bed. His air conditioner was on and I loved that because I hated being hot. Yatta got in with me and pressed play on the movie. He leaned over and opened something on the side of his bed.

"You want one baby?" It was a can of Ohana fruit punch.

"Yea, thanks," I smiled at him. He had a mini fridge plugged up by his bed. I liked that and took a note of it for when I get my place.

"Is the rent real expensive here? I'm thinking about moving into my own place," I don't know why I said that. He probably like 'bitch not in my building'. But instead, he smiled and said.

"I pay a lot but I have an upgrade unit and I'm top floor. I'd love for you to move in the same building as me," I smiled back at his fine ass.

We started watching the stand-up and when I tell y'all the shit was so funny. *Katt Williams* is so crazy and funny as hell. Me and Kenyatta were cracking up. We watched the whole thing laughing and mocking some of his jokes. Next, I chose *Pirates of the Caribbean: Dead Men Tell No Tales*. While it played I got more comfortable in his big bed.

"Come over here, baby," Oh, my God, his voice was so sexy and low when he said that.

With my heart in my ass and my stomach filled with butterflies, I scooted over to him. I laid my head on his chest and when he kissed the top of my forehead I melted. His chest was so hard but yet soft because his skin was soft. He was so warm and his light skin was gorgeous all over. He grabbed my hand and locked his fingers with mine. I smiled to myself as he started kissing my hand then my arm. He tilted my head up by my chin and kissed my lips.

I watched enough movies to know that this was all it takes. Sure enough, our kiss got deep and he pulled me on top of him. I felt his hard dick under me and I was getting so wet. I had been horny before but this was something new. I was not in control of my moans in his mouth and the way I gripped his nice toned arms. He pulled away and looked at me with his bottom lip in his mouth.

"Spend the night with me, Erin. I want to make love to you all night and wake up to you," I almost died when he said that.

"Um, Kenyatta I-I-I um," my palms started sweating and my mouth got dry.

"What's wrong?" I looked at him and couldn't find my words. Come on Erin be an adult.

"I'm a virgin," I said while looking at him.

"A WHAT!" he sat up making me sit up. See, I knew I shouldn't have told him. I shouldn't have even got this far with him. I'm too nerdy and inexperience for him and boring. I couldn't help my tears from falling.

"Erin don't cry, baby. I'm sorry for yelling and scaring you its just you shocked me," he tried to touch me but I moved away. I was ready to get home and bury myself in my bed.

"Come on cutie pie don't be like that. It's just, your fucking gorgeous and the whole fucking package. I don't get how no nigga has ever got on that level with you," I wiped my face and smacked my lips.

"Well excuse me for being a good girl. Would you like me to let a nigga get at me on that level then come back to you? Would that make you feel better?"

"Yo, you better shut that shit up girl! Ain't no nigga about to fucking touch you unless he wanna deal with me. You being a virgin isn't a problem it's just a fucking shock. Now don't say no shit to me like that again!" I looked at him and he was pissed off. I wiped my face again and waited for him to say something.

"Erin if you give me your virginity then we bonded my baby. I'm gone feel like that's my pussy and mine alone. I'm a fucking lose it if I even think you with somebody else. We young as fuck and I ain't tryna lock yo' ass down like that. But me finding out no dick has been up you changed the game. How you feel about that?" I looked straight ahead to gather my thoughts. I honestly don't know how to feel. I had so many mixed emotions.

"So am I like a quest or some shit. If I have sex with you I'm bonded to you for life but if I don't you don't want another nigga to get at me?" I was getting kind of mad and to make matters worse he laughed.

"You ain't no fucking quest, more like a diamond. And in a way your kind of right. You're the whole deal. Sexy, sweet, smart, beautiful inside and out, and we vibe good. Hell naw I don't want you with someone else. But then you turn around and tell me you're a fucking virgin. Meaning nobody has been inside you. You probably only kissed or got that pussy licked," my eyes got big when he said that and he laughed and nodded his head.

"Exactly. So in a way your right. You give me your v-card then we linked up until we die. You don't then I swear I will stalk yo' ass and fuck up whoever you try to be with," I laughed but he looked at me with no humor on his face or body language what so ever. I looked away and bit the corner of my lip. Kenyatta was who I wanted this much was true and I know if he was to get a girlfriend I'd be pissed. Being with him was something I have wanted since high school. I looked at him.

"Don't dog me, Kenyatta. Break up with me first if your going to cheat and abuse all I have to offer," he grabbed me and laid me on his bed with him on top of me.

"I swear to you I would never do that. I won't be perfect because I am a nigga and sometimes we just dumb. But I promise to always know what I have in you and me. Just stop saying you not my girl and stop entertaining that nigga Hayden," I nodded my head and we started kissing.

Kenyatta pulled away and picked up his remote. He turned off Netflix and went to his music app. I smiled when he played *112 Cupid* song and put it on repeat. He looked down at me and kissed my lips soft as hell. It was a sweet kiss that calmed my nerves a little. He reached on my side and grabbed a condom out the drawer. It was big and gold which I guess meant exclusive or some shit. Kenyatta sat me up pulled his beater over my head. He unhooked my bra making my titties bounce out. I had never been naked in front of a guy before. When I got head I had on a maxi dress. This was so different but I was comfortable.

"Fucking beautiful man," he said and started kissing and licking my neck. His tongue was big and wet and felt so damn good. He got to my titties and boy oh boy did he know what to do. I didn't know what I would like or not like but so far the shit was all great. He licked and pulled on my light caramel nipples making me moan.

"Shit baby," my body was on fire and I was ready for more. He must have been to because he pushed me back and slowly slid my thong off. I watched him put it in his drawer where he got the condom from. So I guess he was keeping them. He looked down at my bald pussy and licked his sexy ass lips. When he bit down on his top lip where that dip was! Oh my God I almost screamed. He ran his finger over the top of it and opened my lips to expose my clit. Thanks to sex ed class in high school I knew all about body parts. I also know when I play with myself and mess with that piece of meat I cum good as hell.

Kenyatta slid one finger in me and my back arched. It felt so fucking good that I threw my head back and closed my eyes. Suddenly, I felt his mouth and tongue on my pussy. What the fuck was God thinking when he made this young man right here. I mean I kinda feel bad for all you women out there who don't have a Kenyatta in ya life. This nigga was eating my pussy like I was a five-star meal. His tongue knew where to go, his fingers knew how to work my tight hole and his lips made my clit feel so fucking special.

"Kenyatta baby something is wrong. I gotta pee bad as hell. You need to stopppp," Holy shit I'm peeing all in this nigga face and bed. He about to throw my ass out his shit naked and I don't blame him. I looked down and his wet ass mouth was smiling and the look in his eyes was so sexy.

"That ain't piss baby. That's my pussy telling me I'm treating her right. Do that shit again for me cutie pie," before I could ask my questions about what the fuck I just did his head was back between my legs.

"Ahhhh damn Kenyatta," I had my back arched so high I felt like I was about to break in half. He was working only his tongue this time and it was showing no mercy to my clit. My body was rising higher and higher.

"Its happening again baby. OH MY GOD!" he lifted his head and let all my shit hit his face and chest. I was about to die, I felt that shit. It was the end of me the way I came made every time I ever played with myself seem like a waste. The one time I got head was a fucking waste.

"Damn baby. I fucked you up eating that pussy. That shit sweet as fuck and I needed it all over me. I'm ready to feel you now," he took his boxers off and sat up on his knees between my legs. When I looked down and saw his dick I almost packed my shit and left. It was so big, long, thick and yellow. He was going to put that in me and the fucker was going to come out of my mouth. After the condom was on he got between my legs and started kissing me so slow and sweet. My hands were through his dreads and his hand was all over my body.

"Erin look at me," he said and I opened my eyes and did what he asked.

"I swear to never let you go as long as you stay yourself and stay real with me. You and this sweet pussy forever belong to Kenyatta. Ok baby," as he talked he was rubbing his dick against my clit.

"Ok baby. Sssssss. It hurts Kenyatta," I cried when he slid in me. I felt a tear fall from my eye. Damn it hurt like a bitch and kind of burned a little.

"I know cutie pie. Daddy know but I promise it will stop as soon as I slide the next nine inches in you," *NINE!* I screamed in my head. Holy shit!

"Open up for me baby. Let daddy in his pussy. Fuck girl," he started inching more and more in me. His soft lips kept kissing on me as I cried in pain and then all of a sudden. The pleasure that took over was indescribable. Kenyatta wasn't lying about it not hurting for long.

"Good Lord Kenyatta your dick feels amazing. Ahhh," he was licking and sucking from my neck to my titties. His strokes were nice and slow and I was in pure bliss. This shit was like being inside one of my paintings. All the colors, the live motion of my brush or pencil going across the drawing pad. The rotation I make when I'm working on the detail. Oh, my goodness.

"Damn Erin you feel so fucking good. Bet no nigga ever know this feeling right here. You hear me, baby? Your mine forever cutie pie," his voice was rotating in my ear mixed with his strokes, his kisses, his touch. This was fucking mind-blowing.

"Say my name again baby. Make a nigga's heart drop and say my name," his voice was like smooth satin on my skin sending waves from my head to my toes.

"Mmm Kenyatta. I'm linked to you forever Kenyatta. Sssssss," I could feel tears falling from my eyes. That's how good he was making me feel and it wasn't just his dick. His words, touch and just him being perfect was feeling so good. Kenyatta saw my tears and his thick ass tongue licked them away.

"I'm doing it again baby. It's—Arghhhh," I came long and hard as hell. With his tongue in my mouth, I felt amazing and obviously so did he because he called my name out and filled his condom up. He laid next to me breathing as hard as I was. So, I was no longer a virgin. This was what people called sex. Well, I'm here to say that I am a proud member. My body felt amazing but between my legs was a different story. I felt Kenyatta slide me over to him and kiss my forehead.

"Being with you is going to be live as fuck. I can feel that shit baby," I looked at him and smiled.

"I think being with you is going to be the same way. I feel like you are going to be needy and clingy," I joked with him and he laughed.

"I might be a little selfish and want you all to myself but can you fucking blame me?" he smiled big and we kissed. Kenyatta ran me a hot bath and soaked with me. My poor kitty was so sore but the bath helped. After we got back in the bed we had sex two damn times and I just knew tomorrow I was going to be all fucked up.

Yatta

I woke up to my apartment smelling good as hell. Whoever the fuck was cooking on my floor had my stomach going crazy. I'm taking me and Erin out to breakfast now. I wiped my face and looked next to me. Erin was gone but I seen her romper thing on my recliner so I knew she wasn't out my apartment. I got up and went to the bathroom to drain my shit. I felt good as fuck and energized. Damn, I guess virgin pussy will do that to you. Erin was the first chick whose cherry I popped. I know I may have sounded a little crazy last night telling her we were linked for life. But hell, I was just being real like I know how to be. I would nut the fuck up if somebody else knew what her insides felt like. I already didn't want her with anybody else. Now, knowing I took her v-card. Naw! It's a wrap, she mine for life and that was that.

After pissing I washed my face and took care of my stank ass breath. I noticed Erin used my toothbrush and for some reason that shit turned me on. What the fuck is wrong with me? I opened the bathroom door and walked to my kitchen. Erin fine ass was in there with my beater on. Her hair was big ass hell and curly in two high ponytails. Cute ass! My beater was tight on her body and stopped right over her round booty. Shit, I was getting hard but I know her pussy all fucked up from my ass going crazy last night. Watching her mix the waffle mix and her hips swaying back and forth in my kitchen was getting me worked up.

I leaned against the entrance and just enjoyed the show. She had her headphones in her ear and didn't even know I was watching her. I smiled and bit my lip because I could hear *112 Cupid* coming from her headphones. *Gone and get lost in that shit baby. I'm just as gone as you are.* I thought to myself. She poured the waffles in my waffle maker and scrambled the eggs in a bowl. Erin had my whole apartment smelling so good. Another plus for her, lil baby can cook which was good because I loved to eat. She turned around and was startled when she saw me watching.

"Why you on creep mode Yatta," I turned my nose up at her and she said.

"I mean Kenyatta. Why you creepin' and scaring me?" I smiled at her saying my name. That shit did something to my heart whenever she said my full name. I walked up and put my arms around her waist. Before she could pour the eggs in the skillet I took the bowl out her hand and turned the fire off. She was done with our waffles so I unplugged the maker and lifted Erin up on the counter. I rubbed her thighs while looking in her eyes. As my hand went further up I didn't feel any panties which made me smile.

"Whenever you come in my spot. I don't ever want you to have panties on. If you do I'm ripping them bitches. A'ight?" I said to her as I dropped my boxers. I know I said I was going to let her pussy rest but Erin was so sexy. Her pussy felt like home sweet home and she was mine so I can do what I want.

"A'ight Kenyatta," she said all low and sexy. I kissed her as I slid into home base without a fucking rubber. Shit! Oh well, I'll just pull out and shoot in my hand. Her sweet voice hissed in my ear and that back went forward. I fucked her good in my kitchen and then we smashed her bomb ass breakfast she made us. I had to drop her off at home so she can start painting for her second job. I had to go meet with my uncle and my niggas about this cop situation. Bets believe I was getting up with my cutie pie later.

***

"Ok so look, I did some digging and I couldn't find shit about anyone looking into our operation. I had my boy in evidence look through the incoming and outgoing evidence. He came up dry and he checked twice. I even put in information about Alaric's pops and I came up dry. We all know the both of us got the most to lose so y'all niggas know we both cover up everything and make sure shit is good. We been smooth even before y'all three came on." Emmanuel pointed to me, Alaric and Z. Delon nodded his head in agreement.

Erin and Dreka's dads had been down with my uncle since the 80's. They used to sell dope together in Michigan and Ohio. When Emmanuel found out his wife was pregnant with Erin he quit the game and became legit so did Delon. But they always remained cool as hell with my uncle. Delon used to make it easy for my uncle to transfer drugs by providing cars from his job. Emmanuel keeps the niggas in blue and suits off of us. My uncle trusted him and I lowkey did too. I never got a funny feeling when he was around.

"Now, I'm still keeping my eyes and ears in the streets so I advise y'all not to do any hits in Michigan. Keep the shit in other states and not so close together," Delon chimed in. We all nodded and agreed. They chopped it up with my uncle for a minute. We were set to leave for D.C. in three days and I wanted to get it over with. I was ready to be up under Erin and see if she wanted to go to Cedar Point in Ohio for the July 4th.

"Aye, can we holla at y'all real quick," Me and Z got up to see what Charles and Delon wanted although I had a feeling I already knew.

"What's good?" I asked folding my arms. Z had both his big ass hands in his pockets leaning against the wall. Maybe it wasn't about Erin if Z was right here too. Whatever it was I wasn't at all about to be intimidated by her fucking pops. Cop or no cop, if he thought for a second he was about to scare me he had another thing coming.

"Look I'll cut to the chase. You, Z and both are seeing our daughters. We been knowing y'all for years and although y'all got this hustle going on we both know y'all some decent niggas," Delon said looking from me to Z. I nodded my head and so did Z. Then Emmaunel said.

"Just don't treat Dreka and Erin like this bottom ass

rat bitches y'all are used to fucking with. The two of them are fucking diamonds in a rough so either treat them as such or get the fuck on. Lookin' at the two of you, I can clearly see ya not intimidated and that's good. I like that shit. I can respect that shit. But I swear just as Jesus hung from the cross. We will chop you little muthafuckas up in pieces if y'all fuck over Erin and Dreka," the look in their faces told me and Z that they meant that shit. They both nodded and walked away. I think me and Z both respected it as them protecting their daughters. When they left out my uncle house I looked at Z.

"So, you and Dreka?" I arched my eyebrow and waited for him to say something.

"You and Erin?" he said and when he smirked I dabbed him up and we both laughed. Shit was a first because he never laughed. You were lucky to get a loud chuckle from his big ass. Dreka had him in her palm. I was happy for my nigga.

"What's yo' fuckin' problem?" I looked at Alaric as he was on his phone. He wasn't his goofy self or wasn't telling us about the hoops he had these bitches going through.

"I'm square nigga damn. Why you all in my zone?" I looked shocked and Z shook his head.

"Cassidy ain't fucking with him," my fucking mouth almost hit the floor. Z filled me in and I was shocked as fuck. I had no idea him and Cassidy were getting down.

"So yo' player ass done slipped and fell into some feelings, my nigga?!" I couldn't help but tease his ass. Z was cracking up as well.

"Man fuck the both of y'all! This shit ain't funny! She won't even fucking talk to me man and y'all up here making jokes!" Dog me and Z fell out laughing at this crying ass nigga. On some real shit, he looked like he wanted to fucking cry. We were laughing so fucking hard.

"When y'all niggas are done playing its payday." My uncle came in with some bags. We were about to get paid for the hit we did in Grand Haven. He gave us each a bag with fifty grand in it. Hell yea, shit made my dick rise!

"Nigga you still looking like a lost puppy even though you got tax free money?! Yea, my sister fucked you up!" Even my uncle had to laugh at Z stupid ass comment.

"Fuck yo' over large ass! Big Bertha lookin' ass bitch," Alaric snatched his bag up and stormed out the basement. True bitch style! We were cracking up even more at his ass and talked big shit.

"Y'ALL STOP FUCKING WITH ALARIC!" My auntie yelled down the steps. His ass told on us like a fucking three-year-old.

"A'ight I'm out. I'm about to go get my son and take him shopping," I dabbed my uncle and Z up.

Walking upstairs Alaric big crybaby ass was sitting at the kitchen table eating some chocolate cake my auntie had gave him. I swear he was an overgrown fucking brat bitch. I kissed my auntie on the forehead and dabbed Alaric up. He tried to leave me hanging but he showed love. Jumping in my truck I headed to pick up my junior. While driving I facetimed Erin because I wanted to see her pretty face.

"There go my cutie pie. What's poppin' baby," her bright ass turned red and smiled at me.

"Why you gotta make me blush. Now I'm thrown off my mode," her cute ass joked. I noticed she was putting on her shirt.

"You were getting dressed?" I asked her while looking at her and the road.

"Nope. I was painting the Monet painting. I am more in my mode when I'm naked. I know its weird."

"Shit no the fuck its not. That shit sexy as hell and you are definitely doing that shit for me at my crib," I was dead ass. Her body was something of a masterpiece so to see her live and painting while naked. Oh, my damn that shit sounds hot! I had to grip my dick.

"Ok, that's cool but no freaky shit. Painting only," I gave her the bullshit face.

"Get the fuck outta here. I'm tearing that pussy up

girl. Just imagine you lettin' this dick inspire you and then BOOM! Yo' shit hanging in the Metropolitan Museum!" Me and Erin broke out laughing. This is what I loved about her since day one. She was always so cool and easy going. I can be silly with her and even corny. Her cute ass is still going to laugh and make the shit even funnier. Did I just say, love? I mean like, one of the things I like about her.

"You're so silly and annoying. What are you about to do?"

"About to go get junior and take him shopping. You wanna come?" I know I had just seen her but I missed her. I feel like my generation so focused on being thirsty and pressed instead of just acting on how the fuck ya' feel for yo' bitch. Not my ass, I'm pressed as fuck and don't give a damn.

"I wish I could but I gotta finish up at least half of this. But is it cool if I meet the both of you at your crib later?" I told her I was down with that. This would be Erin's first time seeing K.J. and I knew he was going to like her. Me and Erin talked until I pulled up at Cleo's apartment. I told her I would see her tonight and we hung up.

"Why every time I tell you to have him ready you don't?" I got annoyed at Cleo hardheaded ass. K.J. was sleep so I packed his bag. I wanted to keep him for a few days and I didn't want to have to come back for shit. I walked in the kitchen to grab his milk and bottles. Cleo came behind me and tried to put her hands in my sweatpants.

"What the fuck you doing girl?" I asked her as I slapped her arm away.

"I'm trying to hook my baby daddy up if he stop fucking playing," any other time I would have let that bitch top me off and came all on her face. But naw, I wasn't fucking over Erin I'd rather teach my cutie pie how to suck my shit so she could be perfect in yet something else.

"Cleo, it ain't even that type of party no more ma," I walked passed her to go in the cabinet and get the rest of K.J. stuff. After today I was getting everything for my son to have at my place so I can just pick up my baby boy and keep it moving.

"Since when Yatta. You love when I suck yo dick, what's changed?" I could hear her anger and annoyance in her voice. "Since I got a girl now that's when. And her pussy is what's changed. The shit changed my life and I'm a different nigga," I laughed out loud when I said that shit. Cleo was pissed off and had the nerve to start crying.

"So its fuck me and K.J.? What about us and giving him a family?" I had to breathe in and out before I hurt this hoe.

"Cleo its never fuck my son so get that shit out'cho head. It's fuck you and it's been fuck you. You don't want shit out of life ma. You wanna chase after niggas, turn up with your rat ass sisters and friends and be lazy all fucking day. You think I don't know about you chasing behind Junk ugly black ass! Or the fact that you sucked Sway's dick while I was locked up? You heard both of them niggas came into some money and you were quick to drop K.J. off to yo mama for four days," I shook my head.

"That ain't family material ma. That's a hoe mindset an I don't want no part of that shit. I gave you clout already with you being my baby mama. That's where it stops at. Now, if you'll excuse me I gotta take my son shopping," I walked passed her and her fucking tears.

"You think you about to play house with that bitch and my son?! HELL NO! I don't want her near K.J. or I swear I will take yo' ass to court," this is the Yatta that might make some of y'all crazy bitches reading this pussy wet. I nicely sat my son diaper bag down and walked over to Cleo. I put my hands around her neck with her feet in the air I carried her to the kitchen. Slamming her against the wall I used my right hand and picked up the butcher knife she had in her dish rack. I put that bitch right to her neck.

"Listen bitch, I tried to be nice and walk away from yo' ass but you just gotta test me. If you ever try to put a threat on me talking about court involving my son. I will cut your intestines out your fucking stomach. If you ever call my girl anything but Erin, I will cut ya tongue out and put it on her perfect ass pussy. Don't fuck with me Cleo, I ain't got'em all ma," I let her stupid ass go. It was blood coming from her neck from me pressing the knife so hard but I didn't give a fuck. I picked my son bag up and finished getting him ready. Once I had his shit in my truck I went back and picked my baby boy up. Walking passed Cleo she was on the kitchen floor crying her eyes out. I didn't give a flying fuck. Fuck that hoe bitch and she better stay in her fucking place or else.

Cassidy

"Thank you boos for coming with me to my mama house. I just want to drop these groceries off and leave her some money then we can go," I told Dreka and Erin. Zamir was busy with work today so my girls said they would come. I think he was full of shit with an excuse but he insisted that I not go alone.

"No problem boo you know we got you. I don't have any heads to do until later. Picasso here needed a break," I looked over at Erin when Dreka said that. She was texting and cheesing her ass off. I turned the radio down because I wanted the tea.

"Erin, who is that?" I nodded my head towards her phone. She looked up at me and smiled. Dreka was in the back seat and she screamed.

"OH! MY! GOD! Is that Yatta?" Erin started laughing and turning red.

"Spill bitch," I said to her as I drove.

"I spent the night-----,"

"AHHHHHHH!" Me and Dreka screamed and squealed. I cannot believe what Erin was saying!

"How the fuck you just gone sit on this juicy ass tea bitch! Oh my goodness! So how was it? Did it hurt? Is he packing? Are y'all together?" I had a shit load of questions and so did Dreka.

"Yes to all! Oh my God y'all it hurt so bad but then it felt so good. His dick is so big and thick but his tongue game! Jeez, he is just amazing as fuck in all things sexually. And yes, we are together." Me and Dreka screamed again. We were so happy for Erin.

"Aww, our little Erin is a woman now. We are so going out for drinks tomorrow night," Dreka said and we agreed. This was huge as fuck for our boo.

"So um I have some news to," Dreka said. Me and Erin glanced back at her.

"Me and Zamir are sort of an item," I almost hit my fucking breaks.

"Damn Cassidy!" Erin said because I swerved a little.

"Wait a fucking minute! How the hell did that happen? When did that happen?" I asked looking at Dreka in the rear-view mirror. She began to tell me and Erin about how my brother and her hung out almost every night since high school. She said they never hooked up just talked and chilled. Now, I knew they liked each other but I had no fucking idea it was that deep. Then when she said how he acted when he saw her with her boo. Me and Erin were cracking up and in shock. My brother is nuts! Dreka told us about how he brought her back to his crib and once again I almost hit the breaks. This was so not my brother and if I heard another bitch say this shit. I would never in a million years believe it. Actually, I'd beat the bitch ass for telling such lies!

"Wow, Dreka. Now that was some fucking tea. I mean, I been knew this girl was giving Yatta the wet-wet," I pointed to Erin and she smacked her lips at me.

"I just didn't think you would open my brother up like that," I looked at her as we pulled in my mama driveway and she was cheesing. I was so happy for both of my babies. They deserved it and definitely had their hands full.

"Ma!" I called when I walked in her house. Some Timberland boots who I knew were a niggas were on the floor. As soon as I was about to call her name again she walked out her bedroom with a short ass robe on.

"Shh! Before you wake my nigga up," me, Dreka, and Erin put the Walmart bags down on the table.

"Ma, if you have a nigga living here why can't he buy groceries and give you money?" I asked and she shot me the dirtiest look.

"Because he didn't come out my pussy, he just eats it," I turned my nose up. Dreka and Erin did too.

"And get these bitches out my house before my nigga wakes up and sees them! Why the fuck didn't yo' brother come with you?!" I looked back at my girls and then at my mama.

"Ma you know Dreka and Erin so don't do that and Z had to work," As I talked her bedroom door opened up. Some tall light skin nigga walked out. I won't lie, he was fine as fuck. He looked at me and then at my girls. He zoomed his eyes on Erin and my mama saw it.

"My bad baby. My daughter was dropping off these groceries. Her and her loud as friends were just leaving," she walked up to him smiling but he still had eyes on Erin. When she peeped it shescrunched her face up.

"Naw these beautiful ladies ain't no problem. Especially you," he said pointing to Erin. My mama pushed him back in her room and closed her door.

"Get the fuck out of my house and don't bring these hoes back over here again," she said through her teeth. I just shook my head at her stupid ass and we all walked out.

"I swear all I need is twenty-minutes with your mama and I will beat her like a bad ass child," Dreka said as we headed back to my Toyota.

"I would let you too. That shit don't make no sense and I apologize about her rude ass y'all," I said to Erin and Dreka.

"Girl Bye! Do not apologize for her bullshit boo. Lowkey, her nigga was fine as hell though," Erin said and we all laughed. He really was though.

***

I stood in the mirror and looked me up and down. I was very satisfied with my olive green bodycon dress that stopped a little above my knees. I had on some nude strap around the ankle pumps. The one thing I loved about my short haircut was the low maintenance. Because my hair was so good I just curled the long part that covered my left eye. I had some gold diamond studs that my brother brought me in my ear and some gold bangles on. I was looking good as hell.

Jamil was picking me up so we could go eat at Giovanni's in downtown Detroit. I loved Italian food so when he suggested that we eat there I was down.

I needed a date to take my mind off of Alaric. Speaking of him, he had got a new number and texted my phone to give it to me. I didn't save it I just looked at the message and went back to doing what I was doing. It was a risk being with Alaric. He was used to being a player and playing games. Who's to say that if I take him back he wouldn't just dog me? This might just be a challenge for him to see if he can get me. Naw, I'm good bruh. My phone vibrated and it was Jamil telling me he was outside. I texted him and told him I was coming down now. I grabbed my gold purse wallet and my nude blazer. Locking up my apartment I walked out ready to go on my date.

"Wow, Cassidy. You look beautiful," Jamil said as I got in his 2018 Jeep Wrangler. Jamil was fine. A little on the slim side for my taste but he had some nice waves and a gorgeous smile. He was about six-foot even and dressed casual. He worked at the college as a teacher's aide and cut hair on the side. He was sweet and I had been knowing him all year. I knew he liked me but we just never went out.

"Thanks, handsome. You look pretty good yourself," I smiled at him as he pulled off. He had DMX playing low in the background. Every time I think of him I just think of how fine he was in the movie *Belly*. Damn shame his own family member fucked him up like that. Hating in its true form.

"So, how was your day?" Jamil asked me.

"It was pretty good. I did two girls nails earlier, went to visit my mama and hung out with my girls. How was your day?" I looked at him and asked. He glanced at me and smirked.

"My day was pretty cool. I went to the gym, grocery shopping and went to help my sister move," I nodded my head. We started talking about small stuff like our summer plans, food, and music. Jamil was real cool the only thing was he wasn't a jokester. He laughed but he wasn't into slapstick funny. Like he didn't think *Jim Carey*, *Eddie Murphy* or *Chris Tucker* movies are funny. All three of them are my favorite so that was a thumbs down for me. He really wasn't into comedy shows either. Like who the hell doesn't like shows like *Martin, The Wayans Bros* or *A Different World*?

We pulled up at the restaurant and he opened the door for me. Another red flag was he walked way ahead of me. Almost like I wasn't even with him. I don't like that shit, supposed some shit went down. His ass wouldn't even know it. He held the door open for me and we walked in.

"Welcome to Giovanni's. Do we have a reservation tonight?" The hostess asked. Jamil gave her his name and she seated us.

Jamil pulled my chair out and I told him thank you as I sat down. I was so hungry and could really use a drink. The restaurant had a nice ass turn out tonight. It was getting dark so the dim lights with the dark wood tables and chairs made the feel sexy.

"I'm so glad you decided to go out with me Cassidy. I been wanting to ask you out for a while," Jamil smiled at me and said.

"Really? Why didn't you?" I asked as I looked up and saw the waiter coming towards us. We told her we weren't ready to order but we did order water and some wine.

"To answer your question it was two things. One you brother, he looked like he wasn't letting anybody near you on campus. The second thing was your beauty. It's a bit intimidating," he laughed and I did to. I have never been told that before.

"Wow! Well, my brother is a big teddy bear and as long as you're not trash he wouldn't have said anything to you. And I have never been told my looks are intimidating. Jamil, I'm nothing special nor am I stuck up. If your nice, respectful and treat me nice then I'll give a guy a fair chance," I smiled at him. He shocked me when he grabbed my hand and kissed it.

"You are definitely something special," I blushed and smiled.

"Oh my God," I said and Jamil turned around to see what I was talking about.

Alaric

An hour before

Lately, baby, I've been thinking
How good it was when you were here
And it ain't the wine that I been drinking
For once I feel my head is clear
But early this morning when I opened up my eyes
That old lonesome feeling took me by surprise
I guess you meant more to me than I realized...

I have been playing this *Dru Hill the Love We Had Stays on My Mind* song for three days straight. I don't know what the fuck is wrong with me. I been knowing Cassidy forever and never would have thought she would fuck my head up this bad. I had been trying for three damn weeks to get her to talk to me. I even went up to her job and begged! Nothing. I texted, called, hit her DM up on all social media. Nothing! I don't know why out of all the bitches I have ever fucked with does she have me like this. We spent two months getting to know each other on another level. Laughing, late night texts and phone calls, movie nights and junk food fests. The sex! Let's not forget about her good ass sex.

I missed the fuck out of her good ass pussy. The taste, smell the feel and the sound. I missed it so fucking bad. I just missed her man. Her fucking smile, her touch, her voice and the way she calls me Ric. What the fuck God! Why you doing your child like this man? Help me the fuck out big homie. I was laid on my king size bed just looking dumb as hell. I got so tired of my phone blowing up with every bitch but Cassidy. I changed my number on all them hoes. Only my family and niggas had my shit. My stupid ass dad kept calling me but I hadn't talked to him since our fight. Fuck that nigga right now. I picked up my phone and went through Cassidy's pictures again. We stayed taking pictures or recording videos because I was a conceited nigga and she was bad.

Looking at her smile, her sleep, somewhere she was caught off guard made me want to pull her ass out the picture. I had some X-rated ones I took and some she sent me. Then I went to our videos. We were goofy as fuck with the filters and shit. Our nasty ones were so damn sexy. I got one where I was eating her pussy so good. She couldn't even hold the phone right I was fucking her up so bad. Then it was one where she was sucking the skin off my dick. Her sexy ass lips and little hand around my shit was driving me crazy. Her moans and fucking faces had me sitting here beating my meat.

"Fuck!" I shot nut in the air and that shit landed on my fucking face. Rolling off my bed I fell on my ass and ran to my bathroom. I washed my face off and looked in the mirror at myself.

"You know you pathetic, right nigga? Your fucking lame as hell," I said to my reflection.

Turning my bathroom light off I walked in my living room and opened the blinds. I was on the top floor of my apartment so I just looked at my pretty ass city. Why was this shit happening to me at such a young ass age? All I wanted to do is live my life and have a good time. I feel like everything around me is on autopilot. I just wanted Cassidy to hear me out. Looking at my time I knew the mall was closed.

"Fuck this shit," I said out loud. I snatched my keys off the table along with my wallet and left my apartment. I was sick of this shit and I was making Cassidy hear me the fuck out.

Pulling up to her apartment complex I sat in my truck to gather my fucking words. I needed to get my shit together. I couldn't approach her with my usual approach because her ass would close the door in my face. And I couldn't talk to her like I do these randoms because she might put a bullet in me. I just needed to----My thoughts were cut off at the bullshit in front of me.

I saw Cassidy come out of her apartment in this to tight to short dress on. She walked to this Jeep Wrangler and a nigga got out and opened the door for her. When she kissed him on the cheek I almost grabbed my .45 under my seat. She going on a fucking date! Looking like a whole damn meal at that. Well, guess what, I was about to be on creep squad mode tonight because I was following they asses. I swear to God I will kill this nigga if he thought he was about to get up under that dress she got on. I pulled off with them and kept my distance but made sure I didn't lose them. I sent her text after text just minor messages but she didn't respond. I saw that she read them on my iPhone but she didn't reply.

They pulled up at Giovanni's restaurant and I smacked my lips. Nigga was definitely trying to get some pussy. Feeding Cassidy her favorite Italian food was some points for his lame ass. I watched as he opened the door for her. She once again smiled at him and they started walking to the door. The stupid ass nigga walked ahead of her instead of holding her hand and looking like he was with her. I guess I was happy they were not hugged up because I don't know what I would have did. He opened the door for her and they walked in. I got out my truck and walked to the door. I had on some black Puma sweatpants and a black beater.

It was summer time and hot as hell in the D. I had my black and white Raiders hat on and some black and white Air Jordan 12's. Straight hood shit but I had money and that's what matters. I walked in and told the hostess I wanted to go to the bar. I had a clear view of them from there. I could see Cassidy pretty ass smiling and shit at his stick Stanley skinny ass. Swear I wanted to snatch her the fuck up. He-heing and shit in another nigga face and here my ass is at home missing her. Shooting nut all on my face and shit over her sexy ass and she is entertaining the next. When he kissed her hand, that was it for me. Date fucking over! I walked over to them and since Cassidy's punk ass date back was facing me. She saw me first and her eyes got big as hell.

"Alaric what the hell are you doing?" Alaric!? She know damn well that's not what she calls me.

"Naw, what the fuck are you doing out with this cornball ass nigga?!" I said to her while pointing at him. He put his napkin on the table and looked at me and then her.

"Cassidy, what the hell is going on? Who is this?" He asked her.

"Don't ask her shit my nigga. I'm her fucking man that she been blocking for weeks. This shit here is done so get'cho lame ass on," I snarled at point Dexter.

"Alaric would you stop! Jamil---"

"Excuse me, do we have a problem? You're disturbing other people's dining experience. Sir, if you are not joining them I have to ask you to leave." I'm assuming the manager who came over to us said.

"Hell naw I'm not joining them," I looked at the manager nigga like he was crazy.

"Well, then I'm going to have to ask you to leave," he said to me. I waved his fat ass off.

"Cassidy leave with me so we can talk," two other dudes walked up and told me I needed to leave or they were going to call the police.

"Alaric please stop and just leave. I don't want you to get arrested," she looked up at me pleading.

"Naw, fuck that! I don't give a fuck who they call. Cass love, please just get up and come with me," here I was begging yet again. The two dudes started pulling me out the restaurant.

"Come on Cassidy bae please, man. I'm fucking begging you bae!" I was yelling now but I didn't give a fuck. I was pushing these big niggas off me. I saw the manager in the phone probably calling the police but I didn't give a fuck. My eyes were on Cassidy and she was shaking her head.

"Fuck that lame ass nigga bae! Just come back to me man I swear I'll do right!" I know I was about to be all over somebody's Facebook but I didn't give a shit. I wanted

Cassidy to come back to me. This shit was only seen in movies of a fucking series on TV. Cassidy really didn't come and these big niggas had finally got my wild ass outside.

"FUCK!" I yelled. I started to walk back in that bitch but the niggas were blocking the door. Fuck this shit. I was about to race to her place and wait for her.

I got to my truck and got in. Putting my head back I put both my hands on my face and I wanted to pull my fucking skin off. I was doing shit that I would have laughed if you told me a month ago I would be doing. I don't know how far I was going to go to get this girl to talk to me. All I know was I just didn't want to stop. She was fucking mine. I jumped up when my car door opened. Cassidy jumped in on the passenger side closing the door. I was fucking stunned. I didn't know if she was coming to cuss my ass out or what. We both were quiet as I looked at her and she looked straight ahead. After about two minutes she turned and looked at me.

"Don't ever hurt me like that again Alaric Bell," when she said that shit my ass smiled big as fuck. I yanked her slim thick ass over to me and tongued her ass down.

"I promise on God I will never do no shit to hurt you again," I said to her. She gave me a big beautiful smile and I gave her one back.

We kissed some more and then I pulled off headed to my spot since it was like ten minutes away. As soon as we walked in we were all over each other. I almost couldn't believe this shit was happening. I was just fucked up over not having her and now I was balls deep in her pussy.

"I fucking missed the hell out of you girl. The shit was crazy how fucked up I was over not having you," I told her while I stroked so deep in her good ass pussy. We were butt naked in my king size bed.

"Uhhh Ric boo. I missed you too," her sexy ass moans in my ear had me ready to buss. I had to think about other shit.

"Who been in you? Uh? Who you let in my pussy?" I don't know why I asked her that but I swear I wanted to know because I was going to fuck whoever she said up.

"Nobody Ric, I swear no nigga has oh my Goddd," I could feel and hear her pussy gushing all on my dick. That sweet ass sound. I pulled out and dropped my head between her legs.

"Ahhhhh Ric shit that's my spot boo," I was giving my all to her pussy. I missed the fuck out of her taste. I was even rubbing my nose in it. In case I was dreaming, I wanted to do all the things I been wanting to do to her before I wake up. I flipped her over and went to town on her ass and pussy at the same time. Cassidy was on all fours riding the fuck out of my face and I was loving that shit. Once she came again I slid my dick back in.

"Ugh fuck Cass love, damn you got some good ass pussy girl," I had my nails so deep in her ass cheeks. I was opening them enjoying watching my dick go in and out. Her smooth ass back was in a sexy arch and she was gripping the sheets for dear life.

"You never leaving me again Cassidy. I swear I will kill yo' ass if you tried. Say it, say you ain't never leaving me again," I slapped her pretty ass cheeks making her screech loud.

"Shiiittt Ric! I swear I'll never leave you again. I fucking swear!" I looked down at my dick and it was covered. Once again we didn't use a condom and I didn't even give a fuck. I was just happy to have her back. I fucked her silly until the sunrise and we finally passed out.

***

"Well ain't this some cute shit!" Me and Cassidy jumped up when we heard a loud voice in my room. I looked up to my dad on my dresser with his two boys in my shit to.

"What the fuck you doing dad?" I pulled the cover over Cassidy's body to make sure she was covered. We both were naked as hell.

"I'm here to see my son. My one and only son who has been dodging the fuck out of me like I didn't put his ass inside of his mama," he was pissed off and then he looked at

Cassidy and licked his lips.

"Well damn, I see why you been laying low. She fine as fuck son! My fucking boy!" he started clapping his hands and laughing. He was sitting on my dresser with his all black on and his beanie cap on.

"Dad could you and your niggas get the fuck out?! I'll get at you later," when I said that he started cracking the fuck up.

"Nigga, you don't dismiss me! I'm YO' fucking father! Now, I saw how you laid up with this pretty thing. She got you acting different, like you in love. I can't have that," he pulled his gun out and my eyes got big as fuck. He nodded at his men and they both grabbed my naked ass up and pinned my ass against the wall. Cassidy screamed and started crying. My dad walked over to her licking his lips.

"Dad I swear to God!" I yelled. He stopped walking and cocked his head to the side looking at me.

"You swear what nigga! What the fuck you gone do to me?! I will whoop yo muthafuckin' ass in front of this bitch," he looked back at Cassidy and she started crying and trying to move. He snatched the cover off her exposing her naked body. My dad two friends looked away. That told me they really didn't want to do this.

"Come on dad I'm begging you not to fucking hurt my girl!" he looked up at me smiling.

"Yo' girl huh?" He put his gun to her head making her scream and close her eyes and cry. That shit broke me and I felt my tears fall.

"Nigga, this bitch got you crying for her! Like I raised a fucking pussy ass nigga! Naw, she gotta go." I saw my dad face and he pressed the gun harder to Cassidy's head.

"NO!" I yelled and when I heard the gun go off and I closed my eyes.
PHEW!

Dreka

"Daddy that is such great news! Mama is going to flip when she hears this!" I jumped up and down in excitement and hugged my daddy. The greatest father in the whole world. My mama has a date when she can meet with the parole board. They want to see if she is ready to be back in society. It looks good if all her family is up there to support her and speak on her behalf. I can't fucking wait! In two months all of my family was going to be posted up there begging to let my fucking mama free! Thank you, God!

"Yea she gone wild out when I tell her this. Look, is it cool if I tell her this by myself? I know she gone be happy and want to celebrate," at first I was about to get mad as hell. Why the hell wouldn't I want to be there to tell my mama the biggest news of her life?! Then I looked at my daddy and saw his face. Ugh!

"Daddy that's fucking disgusting! It's cool just take me to see her next weekend please," he agreed and then went in his pocket and gave me a piece of paper.

"Here cheeks. Your daddy got a raise at work so I put some money into your account. It should clear in two business days. Just a little something to tell you how proud I am of my cheeks," he smiled and pinched my cheeks. I opened the paper and it said fifteen grand.

"Oh, my goodness daddy! What the hell kind of raise did you get?!" I smiled big as hell and hugged him again. My dad has always looked out and gave me money. Hundreds at a time sometimes a thousand here and there. But never this much at one damn time. So many ideas came in my mind manly my shop. This is such a good ass startup!

"Anything for you Dreka and you know that. Also, this thing with you and that big nigga Zamir," I looked at him quick as fuck. Oh my God! How the hell did he know about that?!

"Calm down cheeks, yo daddy knows everything that go on with you in the streets. Listen to me," he had a stern expression and I was all ears.

"Don't get caught up in any shit that you don't have to. Your daddy is a fucking true goon, nothing like these young niggas pretending to be. I will kill this whole fucking state for you if that nigga puts you in any drama. I'll gladly do the time while holding my twelve-inch in my fucking hand. Know that always Dreka, you came from me and ain't shit you could ever be in that I wouldn't get you out of. Ok?" I looked at him and said ok. He hugged me again, kissed me on my forehead and walked in the kitchen. I loved my daddy so much and because of him, I know how I'm supposed to be treated by a man. Although I could have gone without knowing how big my father's penis is but ya know that's just his blunt ass. He really is such a gem. I looked at my phone and saw I needed to head to the shop. I had some heads to do.

"I'm out daddy and grandma! I love y'all," I shouted to him and I heard them both tell me bye and they love me to.

Getting in my Sonata I played *Beyoncé B-Day* album and pulled off. It was still a little early in the day. If my clients didn't fuck around then I could be out the shop around five and chill with my bae. I was so happy me and Zamir made shit official. I have been wanting to be with him for a minute now. For him to not do the relationship thing he was doing great so far. I guess we had an advantage because we knew a lot about each other. I knew when he was mad or annoyed at me. He knew when I was having a bitch mood and when I was being a brat.

Even though now I feel we have a whole new way we need to learn each other. Zamir doesn't know how I act as a girlfriend. I don't play about my nigga, I'm jealous and I love attention and being babied. Turn ya; nose up all you want but that's Dreka for you. Speaking of my bae, he was calling me right now.

"What's up Zamir?" I pushed the button on my LG rose gold Bluetooth that was around my neck.

"Don't answer yo' phone like that when I call you Dreka," I laughed because he real life had a attitude.

"How the hell else am I supposed to answer the phone Zamir?" I asked laughing but he was not laughing at all.

"Bae, daddy, boo. Hell, I don't know, not no damn 'what up Zamir.' Let's try this shit again," I laughed hard as fuck when he said that and even harder when he really hung up. My phone rung again and I answered it.

"Hey my mir-mir," I said in the cutest voice. I swear his big ass was smiling, I could just feel it. Big solid sexy ass.

"What's good my baby girl. What'chu doing?" I smiled and shook my head.

"I'm on my way to work so I can knock out these heads. What are you doing?"

"Shit playing the game. I didn't have work today because the gym is getting its plumbing problems handled. So when you get off you bringing that pretty face here ai'ght?" I smiled and bit my top lip.

"Is that an invitation?"

"Hell naw, it's not. That's a fucking request. I better see yo' sexy ass after work *and* you staying the night," I laughed and told him ok. We talked my whole way to the shop.

Getting out I still had Zamir on my Bluetooth. His ass would not let me hang up until I was inside the damn building and inside my suite.

"Ok bae I'm literally inside the shop now. I gotta go," I walked in the back grabbed some supplies for my workstation. I spoke to everyone and saw Tia ugly ass washing some chick hair. Her makeup was extra heavy today. I figured she didn't heal all the way from when Zamir beat her ass. I wasn't even for a nigga putting his hands on a woman. But this was a thot bitch so I felt different about it.

"Have a good day baby girl and hurry the fuck up and

get here," I smiled at his sexy ass voice. I said bye and hung up.

"You mean to tell me I'm out of time on making you, my wife? Damn!" Soul joked as we hugged each other. Domonique, the owner, was here this time. She walked up to me and gave me a big ass hug.

"My thickums diva! As always you look gorgeous," I laughed and told Domonique thank you. She was always so over the top and extra but you loved her loud ass. She was light skin with long ass platinum blonde weave that went past her ass. The bundles were the best of the best and her makeup was always done by the Gods.

"Look at that ass in them jeans! Soul about to bust a big one!" We all laughed and yelled when Dominique said that shit. I had on some skin tight destroyed jeans that exposed my thighs and a peach flared crop top that strapped around my neck. My hands and feet were on point as always and I had my silver and gold bling sandals on. I guess I was on point.

"Domonique you are fucking crazyyy!" I laughed as I sat up my station. I looked at Soul and his eyes were glued on my shape.

"I'm speaking the truth! Look at him," she said and Soul laughed and waved her off. He was finishing up a chick sew-in as he put his beat headphones on. He knew if Domonique was here then we were definitely going to talk about niggas. I watched Tia as she kept rolling her eyes and smacking her lips. Stupid bitch.

"So spill us the dirt baby. Who had my china face doll smiling hard?" Nokia one of Dominique's makeup artists asked. I wasn't about to tell their nosey asses anything. By the end of the day, the shit will be through the entire building.

"Whoever it is must like a whole'lotta fucking woman!" Tia ugly ass tried to crack. Everyone stopped laughing and looked in her direction. She was laughing as she dried the girl head off.

"Now why the fuck you gotta start? You wanna go home and miss out on money?" Dominique asked her and Tia smacked her lips getting mad. Now I was about to be Mrs. Petty Wapp.

"I ain't thinking about her mad ass. But if y'all must know its Z big fine ass," I swear even with the radio on you could hear everyone cough and look shocked. Tia looked like someone just pissed in her morning grits.

"Wait a minute, the mean cocky nigga that be with Yatta and Alaric?! I thought he doesn't do that type of shit? He messed with one of my clients and straight played her ass to the left," Domonique asked smiling but with her mouth still open.

"He doesn't fucking do relationships, so you know her fat ass is lying!" Tia yelled from her corner. She had completely forgot about the chick whose hair she was drying. Poor girl had the towel on top of her head getting water all over her.

"Oh no?" I said as I pulled out my iPhone X. I facetimed him and like always he fucking answered.

"Baby girl, you miss daddy already?" he asked and I smiled.

"Yea I do bae. But check this out, I'm at work and people think you not mine. They think you don't do the whole relationship thing," I hunched my shoulders and looked at him. Zamir was biting his lip looking at me as I talked. I needed his ass to focus! I looked out the side of my eye and could see Tia watching and waiting like she was looking at a fucking movie.

"Tell them muthafuckas to not speak on me before I come and shake that whole damn building upside down," I cracked up when he said that. His face was all cocked up and he was looking pissed.

"As long as I'm out the building when you do that then we good," I looked at him and joked. His face went back to admiring mine.

"I would never hurt my baby girl," I blushed when he

said that.

"Ok I just had to clear some shit up for the nosey people," I looked at Tia and she had steam coming from her ears and head. Looking back at my phone at Zamir he was still looking at my face biting his lip.

"You mine Zamir, right?" I asked and he licked that thick ass bottom lip that I couldn't wait to pull on.

"Hell yea. You mine Dreka, right?" I smiled and nodded my head yea. When we hung up I forgot I was at work that fucking quick. I wanted to leave and be up under him.

"Damn bitch. What the fuck is between ya damn legs bitch!?" Nokia asked as she high fived me. The whole shop started laughing and we were high fiving each other. Tia threw her brush in my direction and it almost hit me but I ducked.

"She ain't got shit but them fat ass thighs! I'm sick of you and yo fucking cousin pushing up on me and Cleo niggas! Take yo' fat ass to Weight Watches and maybe after you lose some weight you can find yo', own nigga!" I cracked up when she ranted the way she did.

"Bitch is you mad or nawww! Imagine a bitch like you thinking you had a nigga on lock and then BAM! A fat bitch takes him from you! Haaaaaa!" I did my Cardi-B laugh with the tongue out! Everyone got pissed and Tia once again tried to come for me and I stood right there waiting for her ass. This time Domonique and Soul snatched her up.

"NAW FUCK THIS FAT BITCH! I'M SICK OF HER! Z IS MINE AND TRUST ME HE WILL STAY MINE," I laughed at her crybaby ass.

"Bitch, please! Sing a new tune and with a new nigga because he is cuffed the fuck up," I told her as Domonique took her to the back room. I pulled my phone out and sat in my chair waiting on my client. I wasn't about to entertain Tia's lame ass. That bitch better stay the fuck away from Zamir or I swear I will become my mother's child for real.

***

I cannot believe the fucking last five hours I have had. So, not only did I get into it with this bitch Tia. But Domonique sent her funky ass home. On her way out this gutter dirt face bitch decided to flat one of my tires! I was so pissed I had to call triple A and have them change my tire. I would have called Zamir but I didn't want him to keep dealing with her. Oh, but best believe I was catching that bitch and showing no mercy. I was on my way to my bae right now. I needed some of him to make me feel better. Then one of my clients did a no-show and the other one was thirty-minutes fucking late. And no, she didn't fucking call!

I pulled in Zamir's garage, grabbed my purse and got out. Walking to his front door I could hear his loud ass game. I rolled my eyes as I knocked on his door. He gave me his spare key but I still wasn't comfortable with just walking in. I knocked again and he still didn't answer the door. I pulled my keys out and searched for his key. Opening the door his big ass was sitting on the recliner playing the game.

"Babe, you didn't hear me knocking?" I asked closing the door.

"I did but I gave yo ass a key to use Dreka," I laughed and shook my head at him as I took my sandals off.
I put my purse on the end steps and walked upstairs to use the bathroom. I had to pee bad as hell and I wanted to brush my teeth because I just had a salad with onions in it. Zamir made me leave my personal shit here when I first stayed the night. After I went to the bathroom and brushed my teeth I walked back downstairs. I was really annoyed with today and needed my bae. Walking to him I stood on the side and unbuttoned my jeans. I took them off along with my shirt. His big head ass was so into the damn NFL Madden game that he didn't even notice.

I stood in front of him and took the controller out his hand. He was about to say some smart shit but he looked at me in my white lace panties and lace strapless bra. I loved this set I got from AdoreMe.com. I pushed him back and straddled his lap. I looked at his sexy ass face for a second and then I kissed him. Finding out I was Zamir's first kiss was so sweet and since he followed my lead he was really good at it. His big ass bottom lip was calling my name and like always, I let his dreads down. Pulling away I looked at him and said.

"I had a very bad day and I need some dick," I unhooked my bra and he slid the straps out. He started going to town on my fucking titties. He was so rough but still sensual with it. I had my head back and my hands on the back of his head. I pulled his head away and gave him the Magnum condom. Lifting up a little he opened it while I pulled his hard-thick dick out his basketball shorts. He put the condom on and I hurried and slid down on it.

"Uhhh," both of us said in unison. I lifted my head up and looked at him while I rode him slow as hell.

"I love you Dreka. I never said that shit to no fucking body but my sister. I fucking love you girl," I swear I wanted to cry when he said that. Instead, I kissed him long and deep while still riding him.

"I love you to Zamir and I promise to always love," he grabbed me by the back of my neck and kissed me so damn good. Then he slapped my ass and reclined his chair all the way back.

"Get that fuckin' dick baby girl. Ugh, fuck! I swear I'll kill the fucking world if I can't have you," I had both of my hands flat on his chest. Felt like I was giving him CPR.

"Ssss shiiitttt daddy! Shit, you feel so good," I leaned forward as he took one of my titties in his mouth and started bouncing on his dick. I was going crazy and I could feel my ass moving like some sea waves.

"FUCK!" We both said coming hard as hell together. I was breathing hard and so was he. I leaned forward and started licking and kissing his nipples. He ran his fingers in my hair.

"It's always the ones with long pretty hair that wear weave," he said and I looked up at him smiling. His dick was still hard as fuck inside of me.

"Thank you bae, I needed that," he smiled at me and we were about to kiss but his phone rung. I looked at it on the end table next to him. A picture of Tia with nut on her face popped up. I looked at him and instantly got pissed off.

"Why is she calling you?" I asked as he held me in place and reclined his chair forward.

"Shit I don't fucking no but trust me when I say I'm deading this shit," he picked it up roughly and answered.

"Tha fuck you calling me for?" his nostrils were flared and nose turned up.

"Tell ya bitch why she going around claiming you she needs to hit the bricks because I'm fucking pregnant!" When she said that I felt like someone kicked me in the fucking face with spikey cleats on. I got off him even though he tried to grab me.

"Tha fuck is you telling me for? I ain't fucked you since Yatta's baby mama got knocked up and you know that! Yo' Dreka what the fuck you doing?!" His big ass voice shook me but I didn't give a fuck. I was getting dressed and leaving.

"You heard what the fuck I said! And tell that hoe that Cleo is pregnant to so relay the message to her funky ass cousin. See you later baby daddy," she hung up just as I was putting my shirt on.

"Dreka I swear to God that bitch is fucking lying. Aye would you fucking stop and just listen!" he grabbed my arm but I snatched away.

"I know this baby was made before me and you became official but I am NOT dealing with that bitch as your baby mama. No fucking way! And tell ya, boy, he better tell my cousin before I fucking do," I went to grab my purse and Zamir grabbed my arm.

"So you think you about to leave me because this rat bitch called me on some bullshit?" he shook his head no. "Naw, I told you I was never being without you Dreka. I just fucking told you I loved you and you think you're about to bounce? Hell no. Baby girl please don't test my fucking gangster on this. I will destroy every fucking thing until it's just me and you standing," I don't know what scared me more. His facial expression or the calmness in his voice. Either way, I still was not dealing with Tia's crazy ass. That poor baby will be motherless fucking around with me.

"I need time to think Zamir," I pulled my arm away and went to pick my purse up to leave.

"Ain't no thinking about this shit Dreka. You forever mine baby girl," I didn't even look back at him when he said that. I just needed to wrap my mind around this shit. Swear this whole day can suck ass.

Erin

"This is so nice. It's been a while since I painted with my muse," my daddy smiled at me and said. We had just came from driving around the city and both felt inspired. Coming home we decided to play some Nat King Cole and just paint. Our big boards were standing up on the art vector back to back from each other. I was sitting on a stool painting and my dad was sitting on his stool in front of me painting. We always did this and when we were both done we would reveal them to one another.

"I know it has been a while daddy and I have really missed this. We have to do this more often," I smiled at him and continued to paint. I thought about telling him about my - half-brother wanting to come into my life. I just didn't want to hurt my dad's feelings.

"What's on your mind muse? Your daddy can look at you and tell something is bothering you?" I chuckled and shook my head. My dad was always on point when it came to me.

"Um, so mom's son Jamie came with her when she came to visit me a few weeks back. He wants to get to know me and develop a relationship," I looked up at my daddy to see if he had any signs of hurt. Swear I will tell Jamie to kick rocks.

"And you think that would bother your daddy because of who he is?" he asked looking at me. I nodded my head slow and said yes. He smiled at me and said.

"I raised an amazing young lady with a good heart. I love that about you but Erin daddy is a grown man. I would never not want you to have a relationship with your half-brother or your mother. I have always wanted that for you but your mother is on some other shit. Off the strength of you, I let her keep breathing," I laughed but my dad was dead ass serious.

"I promise I'm ok with this muse. Ok?" he said as he

picked his brush back up.

"Ok!" I smiled big as hell and went back to painting.

"Oh there is one more thing," I said to him.

"Do I need to smoke before you tell me?" We both laughed when he said that.

"I hope not daddy. You know Yatta right? He hangs with Alaric and Cassidy's brother Z," my dad kept painting but looked at me with his eyebrow arched. I used to have him do it all the time when I was little because it reminded me of the wrestler *The Rock.*

"Well we um, sort of maybe have a thing," I half smiled at him nervously. I didn't know how he was going to act.

"How do you sort of maybe have a thing with someone. You either do or you don't," his voice was so stern and dead on that I got scared.

"I mean we do have a thing I guess. I mean he asked me to be his girl, well kind of----"

"Stop rambling muse. You're with Yatta and you wanna know how I feel about it. Right?" he asked and I said yea. He nodded his head slowly and looked me dead in my eyes.

"If he does wrong by you I will dismember his ass and leave him all over Michigan. Other than that, I'm ok with it Erin. I trust you to know that he is wild as hell but you don't have to roll on his flow. You call the fucking shots," I smiled and agreed. We continued painting, talking and listening to Nat King Cole sweet voice.

***

Dreka texted me and asked me to come over. I hit Cassidy up but she didn't answer. I wanted her to come over so she could dish about her date. Painting with my dad was so fun and relaxing. I needed to finish that Monet for my second job. I was so ready to put that grand in my bank account. Speaking of a bank account my dad surprised me with fifteen grand! I almost jumped through the roof when he gave me that much fucking money. He told me shit was going good and he just wanted to give it to me. I hugged him so tight and thanked him. True daddy's girl for life. I texted Kenyatta but he didn't answer but I just figured he was busy with his son.

"Why are you sitting on the porch like you lost your best friend?" I asked Dreka as I closed the door to my car. She was looking so sad sitting on the porch swing.

"Cause I fucking did and I'm beating a bitch ass as soon as I catch her," I sat down next to her ready talk.

"Oh Lord, what happened?" I asked her. Dreka began telling me about what happened at the shop. Her calling Z in front of everyone and them basically outing their relationship. That part made me smile. Then she told me how Tia ugly ass was hating and they almost got into a fight. I was ready to go look for that dusty hoe when she said the bitch flattened one of her tires.

"That shit foul as fuck Dreka. We beating that bitch ass on sight," I said to her.

"Wait a minute though cousin because the shit gets better," she was telling me about Tia calling Z and saying she was pregnant. I couldn't react yet because Kenyatta's big ass Lincoln Navigator almost fucked Dreka's lawn up. He hoped out looking pissed off and holding what looked like some papers.

"You a fucking grimy ass bitch!" I jumped up along with Dreka.

"WHAT!" We both said in unison.

"You did all this shit just to set me the fuck up! Getting close to me and even giving up your fucking virginity!" Now I was off the porch and he was in my face looking like a psychotic person.

"Kenyatta what the fuck are you talking about and why are you calling me out my name?!" I was pissed off now. He shoved some papers in my chest.

"THAT'S YO' FUCKING BROTHER AND HIS FAT ASS DADDY! THEY JUST ARRESTED MY FUCKING UNCLE THAT'S WHAT THE FUCK I'M

TALKING ABOUT!" I heard him yell and cuss but I was too busy looking at the pictures of Jamie and I guess was his father. His dad was a fat guy who looked like *Uncle Phil* from *Fresh-Prince*. They were talking and laughing together. Then there were pictures of me and Yatta in public together. I saw pictures of his uncle and some other man who I assume is his uncle friend because they were dabbing each other up. I looked at the pictures and my eyes started to water. I can't believe Jamie used me to get to Kenyatta's uncle. But why? Why would he do that and what was Kenyatta's uncle doing to get investigated? I had questions after question going.

"You ain't got shit to say? You just gone stand there and cry like that shit supposed to mean something to me?!" Kenyatta was still yelling. I looked up at him with tears falling from my eyes.

"Kenyatta-----"

"Naw fuck that bitch it's Yatta to yo' ass just like the rest of them bitches. Except you not even like the rest of these bitches. You a fucking opp so you don't get to call me shit!" he yelled in my face. I was looking at him in his eyes and all I seen was hate.

"Yatta or whatever the fuck yo name is! You better get the fuck out of my cousin face. She would never play you like that!" Dreka yelled. Kenyatta stayed nose to nose to me just looking in my wet eyes.

"I would never do that to you. I don't even know what's going on," I said as my voice cracked. He still looked at me with hate and anger.

"Stay the fuck away from me and hope I don't fuck yo' ass up," he walked away back towards his truck but not before stopping and saying.

"Oh and the shit you probably heard from your cousin is true. Cleo is having my baby again and a nigga couldn't be prouder," he smiled at me with a malice look and jumped in his truck. I felt like he pulled my stomach out my and dragged it down the street. I broke down and Dreka was right there consoling me. I knew I should have just stayed far away from Yatta. He was nothing but a bad boy and I still gave him my heart.

To Be Continued…………

PART 2 IS COMING IN MARCH 2018
Keep up with me
Also I know some of y'all are still waiting on Kori and Ronny's book. I promise you guys I WILL write them a book. Like I always say I can ONLY write what's in my heart but they will get a book. Thanks for understanding and sticking with me□

www.Facebook.com/LondynLenz

Reading group on Facebook: Through Londyn Lenz
Author Page: Author Londyn Lenz (I WILL BE DOING RANDOM CONTESTS ALL YOU HAVE TO DO IS LIKE MY PAGE)
Instagram: londyn.lenz.authoress

Made in the USA
Monee, IL
20 November 2024

70749827R00104